SIX LIVES OF FANKLE THE CAT

'Reading this most lovely book is pure joy and fun.'
The Scotsman

'Few contemporary poets have written more rewardingly both for adults and children!'
Times Literary Supplement

In his *Six Lives of Fankle the Cat* George Mackay Brown reaches new heights. As well as other stories Fankle tells of his life as a pirate ship captain's pet and the author, who was born in the Orkneys, neatly weaves into the story something of the lives of the island's villagers.'
Coventry Evening Telegraph

Six Lives of Fankle the Cat

SIX LIVES
OF
FANKLE
THE CAT

GEORGE MACKAY BROWN

Illustrated by
Ian MacInnes

CANONGATE · KELPIES

First published 1980 by Chatto & Windus Ltd
First published in Kelpies 1984
Second impression 1984
Third impression 1986

copyright © 1980 George Mackay Brown
illustrations © 1980 Ian MacInnes

Cover illustration by Jill Downie

Printed in Great Britain
by Cox & Wyman Ltd, Reading, Berkshire

ISBN 0 86241 058 4

CANONGATE PUBLISHING LTD
17 JEFFREY STREET, EDINBURGH EH1 1DR

Contents

To Judith, David and Magnus

The Dreamer

'Four pounds sugar, pot of raspberry jam, box of matches, "People's Friend", pound tomatoes, six oranges, packet of washing powder,' said Mrs Thomson. 'If there's any change you can buy a bar of chocolate for yourself. I don't know if there'll be any change. Things get dearer and dearer.'

It was a Saturday morning. Mrs Thomson was too busy to go to the store in the village; she had the weekend baking to do. She put two pound notes and the shopping list in the purse and gave the basket and purse to Jenny her daughter.

Outside, the sun shone. There was a sea glitter in the croft kitchen.

'See that he marks the price opposite every item,' said Mrs Thomson. 'Oh dear, I think I'm going to get asthma

9

again. It was that ginger cat prowling about in the yard yesterday — I blame him.'

Jenny was glad to be out in the sun and wind, on the mile-long road to the village. Saturday morning was the most delightful time of the week; well, Friday after tea was almost as good. She whirled around on the road, she swung the shopping basket, the purse leapt into the ditch.

'Fancy,' said Jenny, 'if I was to lose the purse! What trouble I would be in! Mam would have asthma all weekend. . . .' (Her mother always got asthma when she was worried or annoyed, or if she saw a cat on the garden wall.)

'I'd better behave myself,' said Jenny. 'I will be a quiet gentle girl. I am a young lady living two hundred years ago. I only speak when I'm spoken to. I am modest and good. Soon a gentleman will drive in a coach to my father's estate. He will say, "Sir Jan Thomson, I have long admired, from a distance, your daughter Jenny. I am, as you may have guessed, Sir Algernon Smythe. I am a man of substance and broad acres. May I now respectfully ask for the hand of that charming girl, your daughter?" '

For four hundred yards or so Jenny was a demure eighteenth-century girl. She tripped along modestly, her eyes downcast. It was rash of a young lady, like her, being out on a public road alone. Fancy, if some stranger, to whom she had not been introduced, were to accost her!

'Well, Jenny,' said a deep voice, 'you don't look much like a gangster's moll today, going along so mimsy-mamsy.' (Last Saturday Jenny had been Al Capone's girl-friend.)

It was old Sander Black. His wicked old head peered over the garden wall of Smedhurst at Jenny. He winked a wicked brandy-ball of an eye at Jenny. He wheezed with laughter.

Jenny smiled back. The eighteenth century faded like a Mozartian tune.

Sander Black and Jenny Thomson shared secrets. They lived in worlds unknown to the other islanders: San Francisco, Greenland, a Pacific island, a crystal fortress on the moon.

Sander Black had been a sailor when he was a young man. Then he had come home to run the croft of Smedhurst after the death of his father. He had been retired for five years now; his daughter and son-in-law looked after the fields and animals. He spoke to his daughter and son-in-law, of course, about such things as seed-potatoes and liquid manure; but the treasures of his experience he reserved for Jenny Thomson whenever he chanced to meet her. He remembered rare things for Jenny — how he had skipped ship in Wellington, New Zealand; the Pacific girl dressed all in flowers he had once been engaged to; the morning he had woken up in a prison hospital in Cadiz, Spain.

He discovered, to his joy, that Jenny had been to places even more remarkable. She had travelled not only in space but in time; she had been in Babylon at the time of Nebuchadnezzer; she had actually been in the theatre in Washington, D.C., on the evening that President Lincoln had been shot!

For a young girl aged eleven, Jenny Thomson had had a remarkable life. Gravely she told her stories, sitting on the grassy verge beside the pipe-smoking old man, Sander Black.

'Well, now,' Sander Black would say, at the conclusion of one of Jenny's rare adventures, 'if that wasn't a most remarkable thing to happen to you, Jenny!. . . ' He would smoke in silence for a while. Then he would say, 'Did I tell you about the time I worked in a circus in Baltimore? I was the lion tamer's assistant. . . .'

Sometimes a whole Saturday morning would pass in this trading of stories. Then, reluctantly, Jenny would have to drag home, to a drab dinner of such common things as Scotch broth, boiled potatoes, fried haddocks. . . .

On this particular Saturday morning, Jenny said, 'I'm sorry, Mr Black, I can't stay and talk to you today. My mam has sent me for messages to the village. I've to hurry, she says. She thinks she's going to have asthma again.'

'No more can I stop and talk to you, Jenny,' said Sander Black. 'I go away today. Off to Leith for six months, maybe more. I'm staying with Albert, my son. Works on the railway. Goodbye, Jenny, I thought I might see you on the road.'

A pang of disappointment went through Jenny. How on earth could she exist without the stories she gave and received every Saturday? The truth is, Jenny was a lonely girl. There was nobody else in the island to share her visions and fantasies with.

'Wait a minute!' cried Jenny. 'We'll have a little talk. Only ten minutes or so.'

But she was speaking to vacancy. The wicked old head had disappeared. Sander's daughter Annabel would be packing his few things into his pasteboard case. In half-an-hour he would be on the ferry-boat, well on the way to Kirkwall and the airport.

She would miss Sander Black!

A desolating thought came to her; it gave her a catch in the breath. Sander Black was old. Supposing he died in Leith, at Albert's house, and was buried with all his treasury of stories; and lay in the grave, his enchanted ear a cold shell!

Jenny was aware of a tear on her cheek. It glittered in the sun. It made a little dark spot in the dust.

'Goodbye, Mr Black,' she whispered.

She walked on towards the village.

She was a young queen — Queen Jenny the Third — whose prime minister, a sage infallible adviser, had been taken from her by a man in a long black coat whose name was Death. How was Queen Jenny to rule over her turbulent kingdom now, with that good old man gone for ever? She walked with slow regal melancholy steps towards the village. How could a young queen like her deal with the bandits in the mountains? The other councillors were young fops — no more than the queen did they know what articles to tax, and how much. Ought she to tax sugar?

There had never been a tax on raspberry jam before, or boxes of matches, or newspapers, or fruit and vegetables. The treasury of Queen Jenny might become quite rich, if she were to tax such things. On the other hand, the poor in the cities might starve. There might be revolution. Oh, how Queen Jenny wished that her prime minister Lord Black was still in the land of the living!

'Certainly, Jenny,' a voice was saying. 'A pound pot of jam, is it? Would your mam be wanting a giant-size packet of washing powder — they come cheaper?'

She was, after all, standing in the richly-odoured gloom of the general merchant's store in the village, and Tom Strynd the merchant was going through the shopping list item by item.

'I don't know,' she said. 'Mam didn't say.'

When the last of the messages was in the shopping basket, and the account settled, and Jenny was eating her bar of chocolate, Tom Strynd said, 'Well, Jenny, and what's new in the island today?'

'Sander Black's going away to Leith for a holiday,' said Jenny. 'He's going to stay with his son. His son Albert works on the railway.'

'A good riddance,' said Tom Strynd. 'It would be a blessing if that old thing were never to come back again.'

Jenny bit her lip. She ought to have rounded on the greedy little shopkeeper in a blaze of rage. (Indeed she would, later, in the solitude of her room, when she re-enacted the whole scene.) But in truth Jenny was a timid girl, who wouldn't say a cross word to a horse-fly that had stung her.

'You've been crying,' said Tom Strynd. 'What was wrong? Did your mam give you a row about something?'

'No, she didn't,' said Jenny.

'Poor Jenny,' said Tom Strynd. 'Now let me see. Would you like to share a secret with me? I'll show you something to cheer you up. Come out into the yard with me, Jenny.'

Jenny followed Tom Strynd out into the yard, leaving her basket of messages on the counter.

Tom Strynd opened the back of his patched rusty van. There, on a sack, reposed a solitary black kitten. It was very young. It blinked smoky-blue eyes, that were full of alarm, wonderment, mischief.

'Is it yours?' Jenny asked. 'I didn't know you had a cat.'

'I don't,' said Tom Strynd.

'Then where did it come from?' said Jenny.

'There's the mystery,' said the general merchant. 'I opened the back of my van three days ago, to get out some bags of potatoes and turnips, and there, in the corner, was *this*.'

'He's beautiful,' said Jenny.

'I don't like cats,' said Tom Strynd. 'I never have done and I never will. Nasty stinking things. What a noise they make sometimes at night, like a troupe of fiddlers gone off their heads!'

'The little sweetheart,' said Jenny. She put out her hand and with the points of her fingers touched the kitten gently. Immediately the kitten responded — it became one breathing trembling purr, it closed its smoky-blue eyes in an excess of delight, it rose and rubbed its jet-black head against Jenny's knuckles.

'I tell you what,' said Tom Strynd, after he had considered for a time. 'I like you, Jenny. Always have done. My folk always got on well with the Thomsons of Inquoy. Ask your father. Well, Jenny, I've grown very fond of this cat in the last day or two. It's going to break my heart to let him go. Funny that, isn't it, especially when I don't fancy cats all that much? But go he'll have to — I just don't have the time to look after him. You know the way it is with kittens, they need to be played with a lot, cuddled and stroked and fed. They have to be trained too. I've been thinking, Jenny. Yes, I spent all last night wondering what to do with this dear little beast. Finally a perfect solution occurred to me — "Jenny Thomson from

14

Inquoy, she's the very girl to own him. She'd look after him well. . . " So, Jenny, he's yours. I'm giving this valuable kitten to you. Pure-bred — I don't need to tell you that. You can see he'll be a good ratter, can't you? Just look at them claws! Have you felt his teeth? Like razors. Every farm on this island would give a lot for a kitten like this. But you know the way some farmers treat their cats — a kick every time they pass them. Coarse brutes! I'm not having anything like that, Jenny, not with this honey of a kitten. So, Jenny, I'm going to pick him up now and give him to you. It'll be a load off my mind. . . . Come, kittums, you're going home with Jenny.'

'I'm sorry, Mr Strynd,' said Jenny. 'It's impossible.'

'You'll never see a kitten like this again,' said Tom Strynd.

'I won't,' said Jenny. 'He's simply the loveliest kitten in the whole world.'

'He loves you already,' said Tom Strynd.

'I think so,' said Jenny. 'Oh, I hope so.'

'He's yours then,' said Tom Strynd. 'No trouble. Take him away at once.'

Jenny shook her head. 'My mother would kill me. My mother hates cats. The very thought of them makes her ill.'

'A great pity that,' said Tom Strynd slowly. 'Because, Jenny, do you know what I'll have to do tonight, as soon as I get back in my van from the farms?'

Jenny shook her head again.

The little bell attached to the top of the shop door "pinged" furiously three times. Tom Strynd had a customer, a customer who needed something urgently, a customer who was beginning to get impatient.

'Coming!' shouted Tom Strynd. 'I'm coming! I can't be everywhere at once!' Then he turned to Jenny and said in a low sweet voice, 'After I get back from the farms, Jenny, I'm going to take this little kitten, Jenny, I'm going to tie a heavy stone round his neck. Then I'm going to drop him in the millpond.'

15

The little bell pinged again, twice.

Tom Strynd scuttled across the yard towards the shop, crying, 'Patience, patience! Job had patience.'

Jenny lifted the condemned kitten in her arms. She swayed it back and fore. She whispered fiercely, 'He won't! Don't be feared, peedie friend. Not a hair of you will be harmed. You'll never see the millpond, tonight or any other night. I'm Jenny. I'm your friend. You're coming home with me.'

It was only as Jenny rounded the shoulder of the little hill and saw Inquoy below her, its chimney smoking, that she realized the enormity of her deed. Who was she to promise sanctuary to a kitten, even such a beautiful kitten as this? It couldn't be — it was impossible. Her mother was bound to find out in time, no matter how cunningly Jenny hid the animal. Her mother could smell out cats — and the smell of a cat within half-a-mile of Inquoy made her ill with disgust.

'Stop here meantime,' said Jenny to the kitten. 'I'm not leaving you. I'll be back in a minute with some milk and breadcrumbs. You sweetheart.' She kissed the little cold nose of the kitten. She put him into an old disused hen-house and closed the door.

Half-way to the croft-house, Jenny paused. She realized she would need all her imagination to get through the next day or two. She sat down on the wall of the kail-yard. She closed her eyes. She picked up a stone. She said slowly, in a foreign accent, 'I am a spy. I have no name. I have a secret number. I am in enemy territory. If I'm caught I will be killed without mercy. I have been sent here by M15. My task: to rescue a very important prisoner, someone with secrets so precious that all the countries of the earth want desperately to have them. The first part of my mission is accomplished. (M15, can you hear me? This is 527 speaking.) I have had success. I entered the prison today. I shot the guards, I brought the prisoner out safe. All is well.

But a worse hazard lies ahead — how to get the prisoner out of the country. Can you hear me, M15? I have concealed the prisoner in a peasant's hut. I will attempt tonight, under cover of darkness, to get the prisoner past the dock and embarkation authorities. It will not be easy. The alarm has been raised. Their anti-espionage people are everywhere. I am sending this radio message from a bleak hillside above the port. I have seen through the binoculars a likely ship. Her name is *Fantasy*. I am returning now, at sunset, to the peasant's hut. You will hear from me once we are safely aboard the ship. If you do not hear from me, then it is all over — the worst has happened — the prisoner and your 527 are captured, probably dead. . .'

A cold voice said at her shoulder, 'What kept you so long?'

Jenny said to her mother, 'Mr Strynd spoke and spoke and spoke.'

'Where are the messages?' said Mrs Thomson.

Jenny had forgotten the messages in the joy and anxiety she had experienced that morning.

'I'm sorry, mam,' she said. 'I don't know what I can have been thinking about. I got the messages all right, and I paid for them. They're safe enough. I just left them, somehow or other, in the shop. I'll go right back at once and get them.'

Such a violent spasm of asthma struck Mrs Thomson then that she had to sit down on the kail-yard wall, five yards away from Jenny. It was four or five minutes before she could speak.

'You foolish ungrateful girl!' said her mother at last. 'What am I to do with you? Does any other woman in this island, or in the whole world, have a daughter like you? I sometimes wonder if you're quite right in the head. A beautiful spy in enemy territory! The Lord give me patience. Who are your enemies, girl — myself and your father? Let me tell you something, Jenny. Let me warn you. If you go on with those stupid dreams and fantasies, you'll come to a bad end! You will, for sure. Listen, girl, I'll tell you exactly who you are. You're Jenny Thomson, aged eleven, of Inquoy farm, in a little island in Orkney. You're a schoolgirl. When you leave school you'll probably work on a farm somewhere. When you're a bit older, if you're lucky, some decent farmer might take you for his wife. Then you'll likely have two or three bairns. Then you'll be an old woman with rheumatics and wrinkles, telling stories beside the fire to grandchildren. That's the way it always has been for a farm woman. That's the way it always will be. Resign yourself to it. It'll save you a lot of unhappiness, Jenny. Whenever you feel those foolish dreams taking hold of you, say to yourself firmly: *No. I'm poor Jenny Thomson, of Inquoy croft.* That'll bring you to your senses. . . . I have nothing more to say.'

'Yes, mother,' said Jenny, 'I'm sorry. I'll try not to imagine foolish things again. I'm Jenny, nothing else.'

'You'd better go back and get the messages then,' said Mrs Thomson, 'before somebody steals them.'

Jenny got up from the wall and gave her mother a sorrowful guilty kiss on the cheek.

'My asthma is very bad today,' said Mrs Thomson. 'There's a good girl. We won't say another word about it. . . . Worst asthma I've had all summer. There must be some cat or other prowling around.'

Jenny crept off once more in the direction of the village, a plain, chastened, rather stupid croft girl.

'A name,' whispered Jenny. 'What name will I give the cat?' As she passed the smithy she said, '*Fankle*. . . . Because, little dear, you have caused so many difficulties already. Your name will be Fankle.'

Discovery

'But where can we hide him?' said Jenny to her father. 'Mother's sure to find him, one day or another.'

Jan Thomson pondered. Then he said, 'In the boatshed. Your mother never goes there.'

So Fankle was bedded down in an old fishbox in the boatshed, with a lining of lamb's-wool plucked by Jenny from the barbed wire, to keep him warm.

'Jenny,' said Mrs Thomson the very next afternoon, 'that's twice today you've gone out with a saucer of milk. What's going on?'

'Nothing,' said Jenny. 'There's a starling with a hurt leg in the yard. I'm helping him to stay alive.'

'That's good of you, Jenny,' said her mother.

The little black kitten grew fast in the boatshed, fed on saucers of milk, and on milk-soaked bread, and pieces of fish and chicken. Soon he was scampering all over the boatshed, chasing flies and beetles and pieces of dust in sunshine. Jenny brought him his milk three times a day. Then she would stroke him, and he would purr like a powerful little engine. 'Fankle's a very good singer,' Jenny assured her father.

A terrible thing happened — Mrs Thomson's cheese and butter were being interfered with! Something was plundering these delicious plates in the cupboard every night. (Mrs Thomson was a very good dairy-woman.)

'No mistake,' said Jan Thomson. 'It's a rat — and a big clever one at that.'

So, traps were set here and there about the croft-house, primed with cheese and grilled bacon. But he was a clever rat all right. He only came out at night, and so nobody in the house ever saw him, and he was so diabolically clever he could get the cheese or the bacon out of the trap without springing it.

'Oh dear,' said Mrs Thomson, 'what will we do? If that old dog was any good, he'd catch the thief.'

The fact was that Robbie, the old collie, who had been a very good dog in his day, now slept the remnant of his life away before the fire. If, on one of his chance meanders round the steading, he saw a rat or a mouse or a young rabbit, he gave it a sleepy benevolent look. Robbie's days as a farm-dog were over.

'Whatever can be done?' cried Jenny's mother. 'Do you know this, the rat bit and scratched into a whole pound of sausages in the night. What we were supposed to have for our tea. And the cupboard door was locked!'

Fankle flourished in the boatshed. He loved scuttling among the lobster creels, the oars, and the coiled fishing lines. He was on good terms with the many spiders in the shed, and with the blackbird that came every morning to sing on the roof. But cats love best of all to be outside; Jenny could only give him his liberty when Mrs Thomson was away for the day, shopping in Kirkwall or Hamnavoe. Then Fankle had a wonderful time between the grass and the clouds. He ran among the chickens, who clucked indignantly at him. He even squared up to the cow, sparring and dancing away, like a little David threatening Goliath. Once he even ventured into the house, and spent a companionable hour with Robbie in front of the fire. He licked Robbie's ear, very delicately. Then he got up, stretched himself, and strolled across to examine with great interest a crack in the kitchen floor, where the flagstone had worn.

Fankle sniffed at that fissure for quite a while. He tried to look in. He sniffed again, and gave a little growl in his throat. Then Jenny had to seize him and run with him into the boatshed, for she had heard the sound of a Ford car on the road. Her mother was returning from the ferryboat.

'Something very strange is going on in this house,' Mrs Thomson complained one morning at breakfast. 'Jenny, what *are* you doing with all that milk, day after day? That bird must have flown away ages ago.'

Jenny assured her that the starling was still hopping around on one leg, and drinking more than ever, but soon now he would be better.

'If I haven't enough to put up with,' said Mrs Thomson, 'with that pirate of a rat! I'm as sure as sure can be that I heard a cat miaowing early this morning, somewhere around the house.'

Her man assured her that that was impossible. There had never been any cat on that croft since they had got married; he knew how much she hated cats.

But Mrs Thomson caught the guilty look that father and daughter exchanged across the table.

'Stray cat or not,' said Mrs Thomson, 'it won't stay here — I can assure you of that.' Jenny's mother was in a bad mood that morning, because in the night the rat had made a skeleton of the cold chicken they were to have, with salad, for their dinner that day.

Mrs Thomson, one Saturday in June, was to be one of a group of trippers. The island branch of the Women's Rural Institute was going on a sea outing to the island of Hoy.

As soon as Mrs Thomson, in her new floral dress and modish hat, was round the corner and out of sight, Jenny ran and flung open the boatshed door. It seemed as if a little patch of midnight whirled past her into the sun and wind. Fankle was all set to have a riotous day of it. He leapt softly between byre and barn. When Jenny looked again, he had disappeared into the long grass of the meadow.

Jenny went indoors and busied herself about the house. She was the woman in charge that day. She would have to make the beds, keep a flame in the fire, prepare dinner and tea for her dad. Jenny loved doing these jobs.

While Jenny was scrubbing the potatoes in the kitchen sink, queen of the house for a whole day, she glanced through the window and got a terrible shock. There, returning over the hill road, were the lady trippers of the W.R.I. They had only been gone a half hour.

What on earth had happened? Jenny soon learned, once her mother was back home, looking so hurt and downcast. (Poor Mrs Thomson, *everything* seemed to be going wrong for her that summer!)

It transpired that Neil Bell the boatman, who was to have ferried them to Hoy, had suddenly been seized with tummy pains after breakfast, and had been whirled away to hospital in Kirkwall, in a helicopter, with suspected appendicitis. And so the trip was off. 'And this such a lovely day!' complained Mrs Thomson.

She was so disappointed that she had got a headache. 'Never mind,' said Jenny. 'I'm getting on well with the housework. You just sit over there beside the fire, mam, and I'll bring you two aspirins and a cup of tea.'

So Mrs Thomson, looking like one of the hanging gardens of Babylon in her summer dress, sat in the armchair beside the fire, and sighed, and sometimes touched her throbbing temple with delicate fingers.

Meantime Jenny scrubbed the potatoes and dropped them, a cluster of pale globes, into the pot of boiling water. Just then she thought, with sudden panic, about Fankle. Fankle, the forbidden cat, was running about the farm, free as the wind. At any moment Fankle might show his midnight face at the door; and that, on top of everything else, might well prove the end of her poor mother.

Jenny quickly dried her hands on her apron and slid like a shadow through the door.

'Girl, come back!' cried her mother. 'Where do you think you're going? There's the table to set. The potato pot might boil over.'

Jenny returned. She said, rather lamely, that she was going to see if the hens had laid any eggs.

'Plenty of time for that!' said her mother. 'See to the dinner. Your father will be hungry.'

Poor Jenny, she laid the knives and forks on the scrubbed table with a sunken heart. It was a house of gloom and despondency.

'No dinner of course for me,' moaned her mother. 'I couldn't eat a bite.'

Jenny returned one knife and one fork into the table drawer. Then she raised the lid of the ramping potato pot. Right enough, if she had gone out looking for Fankle, the pot would have boiled over, and that would have been another sorrow for her poor mother to bear.

'Jenny,' came the mournful voice from the fireside chair.

'Yes, mother?'

'Open the cupboard. See if that rat was on the rampage last night.'

When Jenny opened the cupboard door, she saw at once that the rat had performed a masterpiece of thieving. He had eluded two cunningly-placed traps. He had approached the large round white cheese that Mrs Thomson had made for the cheese competition at the agricultural show in August. Now, that lovely cheese had been protected by a heavy pyrex dish — it seemed an invulnerable treasure inside a crystal castle. The bandit rat had somehow contrived (who knows how?) to lever up the protective glass, and to make savage inroads into the prize cheese. In fact, the cheese was ruined — you could not have exhibited it at a fair of tramps.

As quietly as she could, Jenny reported the disaster to her mother.

It was more than flesh and blood could bear. Mrs Thomson groaned. Two large tears, like pearls, gathered in her eyes and coursed down her stricken face. She was beyond speech. It was all sighs and groans with her. At last she managed 'doctor', and 'brandy', and 'Why do I have to suffer like this?'; and finally, at the peak of pain, 'That was the loveliest cheese I ever made!'

And she looked at Jenny as if Jenny was personally responsible for all her sufferings.

At this point Jan Thomson came in. The two women of the house poured out to him, in broken phrases, the sum of troubles that had happened. Jan Thomson listened with sympathy (for he was a kind man), and he went over and kissed his wife on the cheek, and stroked her hair, and murmured kind words.

'Now,' said Jenny to herself, 'now is the time to slip away and find that cat and return him to the boatshed!'

But, as it turned out, Jenny did not have to go to that trouble, for Fankle presented himself at the open door — softly, subtly, secretly, a jet black shadow. The cat was carrying across his jaws a creature as big as himself, a long grey sinister shape. The beast was dead. And it was a rat.

As if Fankle knew what was what, he dragged his prey over the flagstone floor and, with the greatest of courtesy, laid the rat at the feet of Mrs Thomson. Then he went over to the other side of the fire, gave his paw a long sweep with his tongue, and began to wash his face. (You have to clean yourself well after a battle with a rat.)

Most ladies, presented with a rat, even a dead rat, would have screamed and gone rushing round the room. Not Mrs Thomson. After a first amazed minute, she fixed the grey shape on the floor with an amazed and satisfied eye. There was no doubt in her mind that here lay the pirate that had ruined the summer for her.

'Good gracious!' cried Jan Thomson in a false voice, 'where on earth did that cat come from? Put him out at once, Jenny. I'll take the rat out to the dunghill.'

'The cat is to remain here, beside the fire,' said Mrs Thomson. 'I like this cat. Isn't he sweet? Isn't he clever? To have killed that demon of a rat! I must say he has a nice kind face. Jenny, this cat, whatever his name is, is to be given a saucer of milk at once.'

'His name is Fankle,' said Jenny.

'Fankle can bide here,' said Mrs Thomson, 'for as long as he likes. He looks as if he belongs here, anyway. Pretty pussy.'

King of Pirates

One morning Jenny discovered, not entirely to her surprise, that Fankle the cat could speak. From the very beginning, of course, Jenny had spoken to Fankle, and Fankle had seemed to understand very well what the girl was saying to him. 'Fankle, here's a bit of bacon for you' — that would bring Fankle running from the furthest corner of the croft. 'Fankle, you thief, who stole the cream that mother was keeping for the sponge cake?' — at that Fankle hung his head in shame, and he slunk away among the shadows. 'Fankle, dear, I love you, nice little black thing that you are!' — Fankle's eyes would melt with purest joy, and he would purr under the girl's caressing fingers for an hour.

It was a Saturday morning, and Jenny had brought a

26

saucer of warm milk for the cat to lick at the barn door. Fankle curled his tongue round his morning meal, once or twice, speculatively. Then he said, as distinctly as any budgie, but in far more musical and exquisite diction, 'This milk is from Millie. I've never liked Millie's milk so much as Effie's milk. I wish Jenny would bring me Effie's milk always in the morning for my breakfast. How can I let Jenny know I like Effie's milk best? Still, I suppose I ought to be thankful. Some cats — for example, the half-dozen strays on the hill — never get any milk at all, except when they can steal some. . . .' Fankle sighed, and his tongue went at Millie the cow's milk with a sure greedy rhythm.

'Fankle, you spoke!' cried Jenny.

Fankle waited till he had curled the last drop of milk round his tongue. Then he strolled over and rubbed against Jenny's shinbone. 'Spoke,' he said, 'of course I spoke. I've been speaking for a very long time. Human beings are rather stupid. You think cats can do nothing but miaow. Of course most of them *can* do nothing but miaow. Silly things. But I and a few other special cats can speak as well as you. Jenny, I thought you'd *never* understand me. How very glad I am! Now we can have an interesting talk now and again.'

Jan Thomson appeared round the corner of the barn, driving his old tractor. The steading was rank with noise and petrol fumes.

'I hate that tractor,' said Fankle. 'A stupid blundering thing. I hate machines of all kinds.'

'Father,' cried Jenny. 'Just listen to this! Shut off the engine for a minute. Fankle can speak.'

Jan shut off the engine.

'Fankle, say hullo to my dad,' commanded Jenny.

'Sir, your servant,' said Fankle half-mockingly, half-obsequiously; but all that Mr Thomson heard was a miaow.

'Don't be stupid, Jenny,' said her father. 'Get out of the way, now. I have a lot of work to do this morning.'

27

Again the yard was possessed by frightful din and fumes, until the tractor had disappeared in the direction of the hay field.

'They don't *all* understand,' said Fankle. 'I don't care if he is your father, he's like all the rest of them, very insensitive. Shall I tell you some things about me — where I came from to this place, for example?'

'I know quite well where you came from,' said Jenny. 'I brought you here in my two hands. You were found in Mr Strynd's van.'

Fankle chose to ignore such a common pedestrian statement.

'Marvellous things have happened to me,' he said. 'I could write a book about them. Some day I might. I don't suppose you know, for example, that I was once a ship's cat, and no ordinary ship's cat either, but a pirate ship's cat. You might say I belonged to Mustacio the pirate. Equally, of course, Mustacio and the ship and the crew belonged to me. Mustacio was a nut-brown swaggering man, always half-cut on rum. But I liked him a lot. He was a great success, as a pirate, to begin with.'

'Did they catch him and hang him in the end?' said Jenny.

'Catch Mustacio!' said Fankle. 'Certainly not! Mustacio was far too clever for them. I don't think I'll continue with this story. Clearly you are not interested.'

'Yes, I am,' said Jenny. 'Go on, please.'

'The pirate Mustacio and I first met in the port of Liverpool,' said Fankle. 'I had taken a stroll down to the docks, to see what shipping was in. That was in the year — let me see — 1702. And there, among all the common barques and brigs, was this black coffin of a ship, with dangerous-looking men coming and going. They didn't shout across the water, like the sailors on common ships. Oh no — they whispered secrets to each other, dark intense bits of intelligence. It was clear to me that this was no ordinary ship. The other seamen in the other ships didn't seem to notice — I tell you, most human beings are

28

stupid. However, as I was sitting on that jetty, relishing the dark poetry of that ship, I became aware that two other men were also casting speculative eyes on her. I knew who they were all right. They were harbour commissioners, men trained to smell out whatever was strange or unlawful — for example, smuggled cargoes, concealed guns, wanted criminals. Oh yes, they were interested in the *Esmeralda* all right. The *Esmeralda*, that was the name of the ship. *I am certain of it*, said one commissioner to the other. *I would wager my life on it. It's Mustacio's ship, none other. Listen carefully, Mister Boothroyd. We will act swiftly, and at night. That ship is not to be given clearance before nightfall. Otherwise act as if everything were normal. At seven o' the clock that ship is to be boarded. You are to see, Mister Boothroyd, that the port officers are armed. There will be, I assure you, a fine display of hangings along this same waterfront before Michaelmas. . . .*

'A dark tinker-looking sailor was leaning on the rail of the *Esmeralda*, smoking a clay pipe, and his smouldering eyes were on the commissioners. He guessed, from long experience no doubt, that these two men were no friends of the *Esmeralda*. He guessed, but he couldn't be sure — not yet. Now, I have never been a friend of lawyers and policemen. On the contrary, I am fascinated — always have been — by vagabonds and gypsies and outlaws. I crouched there on the edge of the jetty — I tensed — I leapt softly on to the deck of the *Esmeralda*. I approached the clay-pipe-smoking sailor. I said, "Take me to your skipper. I have some urgent information for him." I'm glad to say that Tomas — that was the sailor's name, he was a Basque — Tomas understood cats and their language. So, in fact, did nearly all the crew, except Sawbones the surgeon, a stupid old thing. Tomas picked me up. He smelt of tar and gold. Tomas brought me to the skipper's cabin. Mustacio lay on his bunk, half-seas across with rum, but drunk or no he was a marvellous-looking man, with scarlet and silver broideries on his coat, and a nose flattened over his face where he had been struck in Sicily by a bandit's whip-stock. And *he*, Mustacio, understood cat language. He listened to what I had to say. He nodded. He kissed me. He gave me a couple of starfish to eat. He gave me a bowl of curds laced with Jamaican rum. When I woke up after that feast, we were on the broad free Atlantic, headed west.'

'How wonderful,' said Jenny. 'I never knew that, Fankle.'

'I could tell you things about Mustacio and the *Esmeralda*,' said Fankle, 'that would make your flesh tremble like butterflies in a summer breeze. Some other time. Old Mrs Crag of Greenglen, she has a budgie I'm very interested in. She lets her budgie out of its cage every morning at half-past ten. Time I was off.'

'But what happened to Mustacio in the end?' pleaded Jenny. 'At least tell me that.'

'It is a brave, beautiful, tragic story,' said Fankle, and his amber eye flashed in the sun. 'Mustacio became a king in the Caribbean. He had enough gold stashed away in chests under the sand to bribe island after island. Besides which, of course, his crew were the bravest sailors in the ocean. They cut a thousand throats to clear Mustacio's way to the throne. Mustacio had six queens, two black, two white, and two chocolate-coloured. He generally had kingfisher eggs for his breakfast. His coffee was half rum. King Mustacio was well loved by those he gave gold to. All the rest of the world of course hated him.

'As for me, I was the Royal Cat. I drank gazelle's milk. I ate goldfish, nothing but goldfish, with a little bit of peacock's brains now and then. I was curled and scented twice a day by a little black boy called Mint. He loved me, Mint. He was so black, when he held me against his black chest I was invisible. And when Mint spoke to me, it was a sweet dark growl, like mulberry.

'I thought such splendour and luxury must go on for ever. How quickly the wheel of fortune turns! The pirate king, as I said, had many powerful enemies in the islands round about, rulers who hated him for his cruelty and good luck and barbaric splendour. These ordinary rulers — men who spent sleepless nights wondering what taxes to impose this year, or whether the flag-ship needed caulking, or whether to hang or reprieve this or that criminal — these thin-lipped calculators formed an alliance against the great King Mustacio. They called up armies in secret. They rigged their navies. They proceeded to blockade the great city of Port of Buccaneers — Mustacio's capital.

'My lord and master was now drunk nearly all the time, and he had ten queens instead of six, fine fat dusky girls that stroked his fat shoulders and stole pearls from his bed-side drawer when he was asleep. Word was brought to his majesty by Tomas — Tomas was Prime Minister now, also Admiral of the Fleet. "The island confederacy have cut our life-lines, Mustacio," said Tomas, with a low bow. "They will starve us into submission. They have landed an army of mercenaries in the northern part of our kingdom."

'"Never mind, pet," said the newest queen, rubbing oil-of-turtles on the vast bosom of the king. "Just wait. This trouble will pass." And the other queens drifted about Mustacio, cooing.

'Mustacio pondered for a full half-hour, while Tomas stood at the edge of the scarlet carpet, sombre and melancholy. Then suddenly the king made up his mind. He threw his queens from him. He got to his feet. By now, what with luxury and laziness, Mustacio had grown as vast as a young African elephant. "By heaven, Tomas!" he roared. "Threaten me, would they? Insult the sacred soil of this island with their rabble of conscripts! The thin-faced prevaricators! By heaven and hell, they'll hang from hooks along the palace wall. Tomas, how is it with our good old ship *Esmeralda*?"

'"Majesty," said Tomas, "she's been five years rotting at the wharf."

31

' "Make her ready!" shouted Mustacio. "Clean the guns — put brass mouth-pieces on them. Rout the sailors out of the taverns. Tell my people their finest day is about to break!"

'Within a week the ship was careened, patched, painted, and fitted with new sails and guns. She was launched. New young sailors mingled with the old pin-legs and hook-hands and one-eyes of Mustacio's original crew. All was gaiety and excitement in Port of Buccaneers, even though food was low in barn and larder, for the enemy's blockade was beginning to have its effect.

'At last the day came for the *Esmeralda*, a splendid lithe powerful ship once more, to sail out of the harbour. I said to Mint, my boy, "Take me to his majesty." So Mint carried me, invisible, in his black bosom. There on the quarter-deck stood King Mustacio in all his magnificence. "Your majesty," I said, "do me the honour of letting me sail with you." And he said, taking me from Mint, "Dear Quichicuto" — Quichicuto was my court name — "dear Quichicuto, you will sail with us. Did you not save us from the Liverpool hangman? You will come, dear cat. You will see what Mustacio does with the enemies of romance and poetry."

'The whole white city cheered as the *Esmeralda* cleared the headland.

'The enemy fleet was waiting for us under the horizon. Invisible signals flew from ship to ship — "The *Esmeralda* has put out. . . . Take your stations. . . . Let every gun be primed. . . ."

'We sailed into a circle of hell. It was the longest cruellest day in the whole of time. The *Esmeralda*, fighting like a wild-cat, was slowly gunned to pieces. The main-mast came down at noon in a flurry of silk and canvas and amber. The grey ships, their gun-mouths flashing scarlet, closed with us. I saw the corpse of Tomas — that brave sailor and prime minister — lying in the stern, with charred corpses all around him. In the middle of that thunderous feast of

32

death, from time to time, rose the laughing voice of Mustacio, commanding, encouraging, defying. Now, at sunset, the grey shapes huddled close about us, and the *Esmeralda* was a floating charnel-house.

'The little black boy, Mint, fell with a musket-ball in his side. I could not bear to listen to his sweet cries of pain. I left him — what could a cat do? — and I went teetering along the tilted ruin of the deck, to find my king. I think, by then, every man-jack on the *Esmeralda* was either dead or mortally wounded. Mustacio had a great gash on his cheek. He licked the blood. "Better than rum, little cat," he said. His right hand was like a pound of mince.

'By now the *Esmeralda* was going down fast by the stern. The terrible din of the guns went on and on, but not from the *Esmeralda*; her last gun had long since fallen silent. "Come, little Quichicuto," said Mustacio, "we'll go now and see what death tastes like. I am curious." He picked me up in his left hand. At that moment the wooden wall of the deck rose sheer against us. Under us was the sea with its salt and sharks and blood.'

Jenny touched the corner of her eye with her lace handkerchief.

'You are not to cry,' said Fankle. 'It was bravely done. And now I want to see what the position is with regard to Mrs Crag's budgie. I've often wondered what budgies tasted like.'

Fankle was away all day.

In the meantime Jenny had been reasoning things out. Presumably Fankle (or Quichicuto) had gone down with the ship. How did it happen that this same cat was hunting about in the hills for mice and rabbits, and was even considering the piratical seizure of old Mrs Crag's budgie?

So, when Fankle returned, just before lamp-lighting time, Jenny confronted him with the problem, face to face.

'Oh,' said Fankle, 'is that what's bothering you? You think I'm a liar, do you? You think I make up stories. Let me tell you, far more wonderful things have happened to me than the Mustacio episode. Yes, indeed.'

'I don't understand,' said Jenny.

'You must have heard — even you,' said Fankle, 'that *cats have nine lives*. Now, would you mind pouring me a saucer of Effie's milk.'

The Cure

The strange thing was, Fankle didn't speak all the time. For weeks at a time he said nothing but "miaow" and "mrrrrrr" and "fzzz", and then he was a very nice loveable cat — not the show-off and the braggart he had showed himself to be in his story of the pirate-king Mustacio.

Not two hundred yards from Jenny's father's croft stood the island church, and beside it the manse where the minister lived with his elderly mother Mrs Martin. It was a sad house, because poor Mrs Martin had not been at all well for years. What was wrong with her nobody knew, not even the island doctor. It was just that the kind old lady was melancholy all the time now. Her sad eyes looked out at a sad world. She didn't see the point of going out any

35

longer, when there was nothing but sadness and vanity to be seen and heard. If she went anywhere, she reasoned, she would only intensify the existing sadness. Indoors there was little solace for her either, though her son Andrew was all considerateness and kindness. Her food tasted of nothing. The books she had loved once bored her now. Sometimes she would take up wool and knitting needles, but all she knitted was an immensely long, grey, scarf-like garment, that grew and grew and was now fifteen feet long if it was an inch.

'Mother,' said the Rev. Andrew Martin one morning after breakfast (which he had prepared and set, for she wasn't interested in cooking either), 'Mother, it's such a beautiful day! There are only two little clouds like white lambs in the sky. Everything is so beautiful and warm and clear. It's a shame to be indoors. You really must sit outside on a morning like this. I'll bring your chair and your shawl.'

'If you like,' said Mrs Martin dully. And she was sorry her words were so leaden and dispirited, for she didn't like hurting her son; and because she loved him, and because the morning through the sitting-room window was so radiant, her spirits sank lower than ever.

Andrew wrestled the huge fireside chair outside and set it just beside the door, and he arranged the cushion. Mrs Martin came out like Mary Queen of Scots approaching the scaffold. She sighed and sat down. Andrew draped the shawl about her shoulders.

'Bring my knitting,' she said.

Having seen her as comfortable as possible, Andrew retired to his study to work on his Sunday sermon, and the old lady was alone.

And really, it was such a beautiful morning! A blackbird sang from the garden wall, burst after burst of purest ecstasy! The two little clouds like lambs had been joined by a third, high up in the intense blue sky, but they seemed to be too tranced with delight to move. The sea,

36

between the two green hills, shimmered. You could almost feel the joy of the grass growing, and the teeming wildflowers. You could, if you were not Mrs Martin. She sat there, the sole blight on this happy summer world. As she sat, a tear welled in her eye — melancholy's answer to the dewdrop in the heart of the garden rose.

She took up her knitting needles, but they made an ugly "clack-clack" in the delicate web of sound that lay over the island. She dropped them again.

Just then, Mrs Martin saw a black cat on the garden wall, magnified and distorted by the unfallen tears in her eyes. Of course, it was the cat of Inquoy, Jan Thomson's croft. What was its name now — Flannel? Funnel? Mrs Martin couldn't quite remember. Some funny name like that. And it was a strange cat too. It followed the Thomson girl to school most mornings. It had (so she'd heard) attacked the coastguard's Alsatian dog — flown in his face like a black whirlwind, claws and teeth out — and sent the huge powerful dog home with his tail between his legs. And here it was now, on the garden wall of the manse. That had never happened before.

The cat seemed to be taking a friendly interest in the creature he shared the wall with — the joyous blackbird. The blackbird was too busy keeping a wary eye on the cat to sing now. It quivered on the wall, poised for flight, should that sinister shadow make one move.

'Really,' thought Mrs Martin, 'if there is to be any "nature red in tooth and claw" in this garden, I'll call Andrew to take me inside. I just *couldn't* stand that!'

And then she realized that the black cat was looking at her, in a very concerned way. He looked, and looked, and then leapt softly from the wall on to the lawn, and approached her.

The blackbird resumed its song, a magnificent fount of celebration.

You would almost think the cat had some kind of message for Mrs Martin. But in the long garden there were so many distractions. First it was the butterflies. Three of them exploded silently out of the rosebush over Fankle's face. He fought with them for several seconds, but butterflies are much harder to fight against than dogs, and the butterflies separated, drifting airily each his own way. Fankle didn't seem to mind such a lyrical defeat. Once more he turned a serious regard on poor afflicted Mrs Martin.

What now — whatever was the creature doing now? He seemed to have found something in the long grass. Delicately he howked it out with a fore-paw, and it was — a fragment of cherry-cake! Mrs Martin was *astonished*. The duplicity of Andrew! So this was what he did in the garden, late in the evening, after she was in bed — eat cherrycake — slice after slice of it, she wouldn't wonder. The thing was, Andrew had become worried last winter that "he was digging his grave with his teeth". It was sweet things that he had always gone for, from his childhood up — chocolate, cream buns, meringues, honey and bread, but chiefly and most of all: *cherry-cake*. Cherry-cake was the chief villain in the thrilling drama that was going on in Andrew's body. Cherry-cake he loved passionately and devotedly — and it was cherry-cake that would finish Andrew off. So Andrew believed. It was true, he seemed to be getting fatter with every month that passed, and he was deeply worried about it. Last winter Andrew had come to a solemn decision — no more sweet things for him. He renounced them, he put them behind him. He got a diet sheet from the doctor which he studied carefully. Above all, cherry-cake, that had been his joy and delight, was to be banned forever from the manse.

Be sure your sins will find you out! So this was what Andrew did night after night, in the garden, when he was supposed to be studying the growth of potatoes and lettuce and strawberries — he was wolfing down, in secret, thick slices of cherry-cake!

Mrs Martin didn't know whether to laugh or cry. If it

had been a really serious business — if Andrew was indeed cherry-caking himself to death — there would have been cause for tears. But the truth was, Andrew was and had always been an acute hypochondriac, forever worried about his health. The island doctor had assured Mrs Martin, privately, that there was nothing wrong with Andrew — he could eat, with safety, as much cherry-cake as he wanted. And Mrs Martin had told the doctor in return that stoutness ran in the family: Andrew's father and uncle and grandfather had been even huger than Andrew: vast men, that set the earth trembling under their feet.

It had taken this cat to discover Andrew's innocent deceit. A fair fragment of cherry-cake Andrew must have dropped and not found in the twilight of last night! The black cat swallowed the cherry, his eyes melting with sheer sensuous delight.

'You *are* a strange cat,' said Mrs Martin out loud. The blackbird agreed with her, thrillingly. Fankle himself seemed to acquiesce. He approached the invalid obliquely, across the shallot bed.

Then, before Mrs Martin was aware of it, he pounced! He pushed the ball of grey wool away, he parried, dancingly he threatened it — you would think he both loved and hated it. Then something happened: his claw got hooked in the endless scarf that Mrs Martin was knitting, and he could not get the paw free. He tugged, he pulled. The knitting needles fell with a tiny clatter on the flagstones. Fankle whirled about, and that was the worst thing he could have done, for the scarf began to drape itself about him, and the harder the cat tugged and struggled, the closer he was wound. The struggle to escape went on for the duration of two blackbird songs, and at the end of it Fankle lay there on the grass at Mrs Martin's feet like a badly-put-together Egyptian mummy. Even his head was covered — one ear only stuck out. At last, from inside the grey swathe, emerged a tiny "miaow".

'Andrew,' cried Mrs Martin.

Her stout son was there in five seconds, his pen in his hand.

'Free that cat, Andrew,' said Mrs Martin.

'Good gracious!' said Andrew. 'How on earth did this happen?' And then, when he had unwound Fankle and unhooked the claw, 'Why, it's the Thomsons' cat — Fankle.'

'Fankle, is that its name?' said Mrs Martin. 'Well, Andrew, since you've been so good as to free Fankle, you can have a thick slice of cherry-cake.'

At the gape of guilty astonishment Andrew gave, she began to laugh: first a slow smile, then a reluctant chuckle, then a full-throated shout of merriment. It was just like the happy Mrs Martin of seven years ago, before the melancholy had come on her. It was, to Andrew, the most beautiful sound in all that summer of music and poetry.

As for Fankle, he gathered himself together with dignity, and left the garden without another glance at Mrs Martin and the Rev. Andrew Martin. He even ignored the blackbird.

It would be wrong to say that Mrs Martin was entirely cured of her depressions from that day on. She still sighed occasionally, and thought with sadness of the emptiness of existence and the pain of life. But she could go out — a thing that had never happened for seven years. She could visit the crofts, and speak to the old women and the children. She could shop at the village store. She sat once more in her pew in the kirk on Sundays. The whole island was the better of that, because they had always liked Mrs Martin.

Every Friday afternoon a little box was delivered at the door of Inquoy croft, addressed in Mrs Martin's writing to *FANKLE THOMSON*. Inside was a tin of salmon, Fankle's favourite food. At tea-time on Fridays, Fankle ate with great luxury.

Rev. Andrew Martin resumed his eating of cherry-cake publicly, and grew rather fatter, but it suited him; and now he didn't mind so much, when there was laughter once more across the breakfast table at the manse.

Little Thief with the Whiskers
that Eats Fish Fins

'Of course,' said Fankle, 'that business with Mustacio was nothing. I had seen far greater times.'

'Is that so?' said Jenny.

They were sitting in the kitchen of Inquoy croft, on a Saturday afternoon. Outside, it was as grey and cold and wet as an old dishcloth. Jenny's father was working in the barn; Mrs Thomson had had to go to the village for messages. Jenny herself had intended to pass the afternoon with a book, but she couldn't get on with it, for Fankle kept rubbing against her intent head, purring and miaowing alternately, and once he even walked across the spread pages. It was obvious that Fankle didn't want his friend to read; at least, not for the moment.

Then he suddenly spoke, for the first time in a month.

41

In a way Jenny was glad, because sometimes she wondered whether she hadn't dreamed the story of the pirate king Mustacio. She hadn't dared to tell her parents, or her friends, or the teacher. Sometimes she wondered whether she oughtn't to tell old Mrs Martin up at the manse, for Mrs Martin knew how clever Fankle was. One day she might tell her; but not until Fankle had spoken again.

Jenny sighed, smiled, and closed her book.

'Have you ever wondered,' said Fankle, 'where I come from really?'

'Well,' said Jenny, 'I thought at first you came from Tom Strynd's grocery van. But it seems you're a Liverpool cat — or so you said.'

'I am *not*,' said Fankle. 'I lived for a time in Liverpool, that's all. I had come down in the world.'

'Is that so?' said Jenny.

'I'll give you three guesses,' said Fankle, 'as to the place of my origin.'

After a pause, Jenny said, 'Paris', for Fankle had a certain style and sophistication about him.

'Wrong,' said Fankle. 'It's true, I lived in Paris for a while. I belonged to Marie Antoinette's fourth lady of the bedchamber. But I didn't come from there.'

'Maybe, Peru,' said Jenny.

'You're just making wild guesses,' said Fankle. 'Every girl of intelligence knows that cats — the best strain of cat, that is — come from Egypt.'

'I suppose,' said Jenny, with a touch of sarcasm, 'you belonged to Cleopatra's toilet-mistress.'

'No, I didn't,' said Fankle. 'I lived thousands of years before Cleopatra. As a matter of fact it was a rather humble beginning I had in life. First thing I remember, I was a little thin cat wandering about on the mudflats of the Nile, eating maybe a stranded fish now and then. Nobody in Egypt seemed to like cats at that time. I got more kicks than ha'pennies.'

'Poor Fankle,' said Jenny.

'I wasn't called Fankle then either. I had a name you couldn't pronounce. It means this, roughly — "little thief with the whiskers that eats fish fins". I didn't mind. I had faith in myself. I knew that in the end all those peasants and fishermen would be forced to call me by a better name.'

'And did they?' asked Jenny.

'Don't rush me,' said Fankle. 'All in good time. Just listen.'

'I *am* listening,' said Jenny. 'But you'd better hurry. Mother might be back from the shops at any minute.'

'One day,' said Fankle, 'as I was slouching along the left bank of the Nile, I heard singing from the Temple of the Sun God, a chant. As you know, I have a very poor opinion of the human voice as a lyrical instrument, but I paused and listened for a while to this choir of men and boys. Usually their hymns were as gay and cheerful as human beings can manage, but this piece was full of the most awful desolation. It was a sponge dripping with pain and grief and terror that they offered to the sun's benign golden eye. What could be the matter? The provinces were at peace. The harvest had been gathered in and it was a plenteous one. As far as I knew, there was no plague in the city. So I said to the priest's dog, who was squatting at the temple door and blinking his stupid eye, "Hound," I said, "what's got into them?"

' "Go away," said the dog. "Be off. Or I'll tear you limb from limb, Little-thief-with-the-whiskers-that-eats-fish-fins."

'Who could be bothered reasoning with a churl like that?' said Fankle. 'Not me. I strolled down to the reeds and I said to the monkey that was sitting on a rock there, "What's eating them?" I said. "They're in a blue funk about something."

' "Haven't you heard?" said the monkey, whose name was Flower-face. "It's the rats from Persia, the new strain. That's what's biting them."

43

' "I thought," said I, "that the official poisoners with their thousand different kinds of venom could easily deal with a tribe of rats."

' "That's where you're wrong," said Flower-face. "Because this rat, you see, from Persia, eats the poisons and seems to thrive on them. Of course they like corn better, and now they've taken up residence in the great granaries."

' "Good luck to them," I said. You must understand, Jenny, at that time there was no ill-feeling between rats and cats. None at all. We went our separate ways. We left each other alone. The only animals we cats disliked were dogs.'

'I never knew that,' said Jenny. 'I thought — '

'What you thought or think is irrelevant to this story,' said Fankle. 'You are ruining the story with your interruptions.'

'I'm sorry, I'm sure,' said Jenny.

'To continue,' said Fankle. 'It seemed, from what Flower-face told me, that the entire nation of Egypt was threatened with starvation. The Persian rats had got into their granaries. They were devouring everything. They were breeding like arithmetic gone mad.'

'How terrible!' said Jenny.

'Terrible for human beings,' said Fankle. 'Nice for rats. It had nothing to do with me. I could always get my bit of fish out of the river. . . . Well, now, that same afternoon as I was sitting on a wall giving my face a bit of a wash, along come three councillors of the city, very grave and important men. They stopped right in front of me. It looked like business. This was the first time human beings had ever tried to negotiate with me, except in the way of kicks, insults, and the flinging of stones.

'The oldest senator addressed me. "Little-thief-with-the-whiskers-that-eats-fish-fins, a word with you."

' "When I have a better name," I said, "I will speak with you. Not before." Nobody likes being called a thief, really.

'The councillors turned their backs on me and conferred

in whispers. Then they turned again to face me. "We have a new name for you," they said. "It is this: Little-subtle-one-with-the-bright-claw-that-will-sit-at-our-fires."

' "That's better," I said. "That sounds very promising as far as my future is concerned. What do you want me for?"

' "You must have heard about the Persian rats," said old white-beard.

' "Yes, I have," I said. "They are said to be very clever, very hungry animals. They eat poison along with corn and seem to enjoy the mixture. These rats will go far."

' "They will destroy the greatest civilization on earth," said the senators. "They will eat the manuscripts of most ancient wisdom. They will destroy all things beautiful and good."

' "Yes," I said, "they are very efficient."

'Jenny, dear friend, to cut a long story short, these wise men made certain proposals to me; and through me, of course, to the whole species "cat". It was this: that the cats of Egypt should suddenly declare war on those voracious corn-eating rats, and root them out, and thereby ensure that men and women and children could eat their bread in peace, for ever and ever. . . . Of course I saw to it there was another side to the bargain. My name from that day on was to be, I decided, Little-happy-and-subtle-one, friend-of-households, drinker-from-fireside-bowls.

'Once the bargain had been signed and sealed, I went into swift action. I summoned a cat congress. They came to Thebes from all over Egypt — tall cats, one-eyed cats, scented cats, skinny cats, cats without tails, hill cats, river cats, sand cats. Once I had explained to the vast concourse the new compact as between cats and men, they responded with a wild enthusiastic huzzah of "miaows". I think I have never heard such a thrilling sound. Thenceforth cats were no more to be scavengers and outcasts — they were to lead easy pampered lives, they were to be the well-loved friends of mankind, especially girls and boys.

'But first, of course, the war had to be fought. We entered the great state granaries secretly, at night. You know what a marvellous place a barn is, with all its fragrance and heaviness of stored corn. In the darkness, the army of cats heard a steady grinding and gnawing, a rustling and belching. The Persian rats didn't want to waste time sleeping, when all that corn was to be eaten. For many of them — for most of them — for all but a handful of them, it was to be their last meal on earth. The cats' eyes gleamed like jewels throughout the granary. I gave the signal. We flung ourselves on the despoilers. They did the best they could. (Rats are very brave and fierce.) But they were crammed with corn, and besides they were unprepared for such a subtle secret massive assault. When dawn broke over the dunes and pyramids, the battle was all but over. There remained only a few stragglers to be rounded up. A huge pit was dug in the desert by a band of slaves, and there the rats were buried, grey layer upon layer of them. It was a joyous hymn that the choir sang in the temple that morning.

'Jenny, I hate to run down human beings in front of you, but there were actually some of them, including one of the three councillors that had come to me in the first place, who wanted now to renege on the treaty. Of course, knowing men the way I did, I had made certain provisions for that. Just when one of those citizens was in the middle of addressing me by my old name, Little-thief-with-the-whiskers-that-eats-fish-fins, I happened to remark, "Look at those two little lovely rats over there playing by the sewer, a male and a female! They should have a growing family quite soon now." For you see, I had kept half-a-dozen rats alive, just to encourage the citizens. Then, and only then, was the treaty implemented. All the cats of Egypt were allocated homes — each one was adopted by a family — and the children of the household and the household cat quickly became friends. And that's the way it has been ever since.

'I found myself, Jenny, being gathered into firm slim

brown beautiful arms. A face looked down at me so kind and sweet and happy my heart melted to her. I would have loved her even if she had been a beggar. I knew she was no beggar, by the silver and emerald rings on her arm, and the fine embroideried linen of her kilt. That was all she wore. And her hair was black and her eyes slanted like fish in a tank and she had a deep cleft in her chin. Her breath was all roses and honey. The princess, whose name means "She-who-will-bake-cakes-for-the-poor", took me to her father's big white house. She poured me out a bowl of milk beside the fire. She kissed me. She said, "You are to have a new name from now on. It is "Little-subtle-friend-of-princesses, with-coat-of-midnight-and-eyes-like-diamonds".'

'Oh dear,' said Jenny after a while, 'what a come-down for you to have a name like Fankle and to live in a little stone croft in an island!'

Fankle rubbed gently against his friend's wrist. He purred, 'Jenny, I like you every bit as much as I liked that Egyptian princess.'

Jenny stroked the black head. 'Oh, well,' she said smiling, 'thank you for saying that, Fankle.'

They heard the car stopping on the road outside. 'Quick, tell me before mother comes,' said Jenny, ' — how did you get from Thebes to Liverpool?'

'By the way of extinction,' said Fankle. 'The princess's cousin, a bad jealous girl called Green Eyes, threw me down a well in the palace yard. Of course I was an old cat then, and tired. I no longer liked fish and milk as much as I had done. I was glad enough to let the water cover my head. Death is sweet, Jenny, once you know that when you wake up from the dark sleep you will be young again, and in a new place, and full of curiosity about everything.'

Roses and Moonlight

A very worrying thing indeed happened just before harvest. Fankle vanished. Jenny was quite prepared to have her treasure disappear for a day and a night. That happened quite often when the hunting mood was on him. Then he would drag home, his tummy tight as a drum with surfeit of mouse, bird, or rabbit — lie down on the rug before the fire — groan once or twice and go to sleep.

But this was the third day that Fankle was not seen creeping through the fields of Inquoy, or sitting in the barn door. The milk in his bowl turned sour. Jenny searched every corner and outhouse for him. Nothing. It was a serious business.

'No,' cried the children in the island school, 'we haven't seen Fankle.' They were perturbed too. They all liked

48

Fankle, even though he had scratched most of them at one time or another.

On Friday, after tea, Jenny could bear it no longer. (And she didn't eat much of a tea either, a half slice of bread and butter with a sprinkling of sugar on it.) She decided to go and make enquiries.

The obvious person to go to, first of all, was Ma Scad, who kept a dozen cats and knew as much about the movements of cats as mariners did about tides and astronomers the drift of the stars.

'Lost him, have you?' said Ma Scad in the door of Troddale, her cottage. 'Is that a fact? Come in, lass. Dear, dear me. It has happened before. The world is full of wickedness. What a sad thing, your cat gone a-missing! What did you say his name was? Fankle. Poor Fankle! Yes, I know Fankle. He's been up here visiting my beauties more than once. A brave cat.'

The dark interior of Troddale seemed to be full of soft gliding shapes, and brilliant eyes. 'Cats,' said Ma Scad, 'have you seen Jenny's cat? Have any of you seen Fankle? Speak up, now. There's not a moment to be lost.'

There was not a murmur from any of Ma Scad's cats. They looked at her with large wise inscrutable eyes. 'They know nothing,' Ma Scad assured Jenny. 'If they did they'd have told me.' (Indeed it was said in the island that Ma Scad had long talks with her cats and sometimes a singsong or a quiz game. But Jenny did not believe that — only Fankle, of all the cats on earth, could talk.)

'They haven't seen sight or sign of Fankle,' said Ma Scad. 'Let me see now.' She leaned her head to one side, narrowed her eyes, put three fingers of her right hand into her mouth, and pondered. 'Cat soup,' she said at last.

'Beg pardon?' said Jenny.

'There's a certain person in this island that makes cat soup. He'll eat no soup but cat soup. I'm mentioning no names. What colour was Fankle?'

'Black,' said Jenny.

49

'Oh, dear,' said Ma Scad, 'that's bad. That's very bad. This party eats nothing but the soup of black cats. Look for cat bones in a certain midden as you go home. I'm mentioning no names.'

'That's impossible, surely!' cried Jenny.

'Then there are folk that hate cats,' said Ma Scad. 'There are. A certain other party hunts cats with his shot-gun. He hunts them over the hill and along the shore. No cat has ever harmed him or his. He shoots cats to please his evil heart. Black cats, that's the ones he likes best of all to shoot.'

'Who is he?' asked Jenny.

'No names,' said Ma Scad. 'I don't want to get into trouble, lawyer's letters and all that kind of thing. I saw him with his blunderbuss no later than yesterday. Fankle is lying full of shot-gun pellets in a ditch.'

Jenny began to cry softly. The dozen cats of Ma Scad looked as if it was all the same to them whether she laughed or cried or sang *Three Blind Mice*.

'Tears'll not get Fankle back,' said Ma Scad. 'You'll just have to learn to carry on without Fankle. Life is very hard. You must be brave. I'll make you a cup of tea.'

'No, thank you,' wept Jenny.

'Let me see,' said Ma Scad, adopting once more her meditative stance. 'Let me see now. Who was it told me? I believe it was Walter the fisherman. No, it wasn't. It was Scroggie the beach-comber. Why didn't I think of that first of all? I'm getting old. Scroggie told me, none other. Alas!'

'What did Scroggie say?' asked Jenny in a little damp whisper.

'Scroggie found a sack with the neck tied with string. Scroggie took his knife to it. What do you think Scroggie found in the sack?'

'I couldn't say,' said Jenny.

'I'll tell you what Scroggie found,' said Ma Scad. 'A black cat. Dead and salt and stiff. So Scroggie told me. And Scroggie tells the truth more often than not.'

'Will Scroggie still have the body?' said Jenny. 'I would know Fankle if I saw him, dead or alive.'

'What Scroggie would have done is this,' said Ma Scad. 'He would have made a fire and he would have burned the cat on the shore. If you were to go down to the beach —'

But Jenny could take no more of this kind of talk. She ran out of Troddale without so much as a thanks or a goodbye. By good luck, half way down to the shore she met Scroggie himself. Scroggie regarded her with a kind eye. 'Please, Scroggie,' she said, 'is it true that you found a black cat dead on the shore, in a sack, and burned him?'

'No, dear,' said Scroggie. 'I never found any black cat. Is it Ma Scad that told you? According to Ma Scad, I find a hundred drowned cats a week down at the shore. I think I've maybe found one in my time, years ago. Is it Fankle you're worried about? He'll turn up, never fear. That Fankle of yours is not the vanishing kind.'

Jenny knocked at the door of the merchant's house in the village. The store was locked for the night. Tom Strynd listened to Jenny's story with a long face. Had Fankle maybe got tired of her and Inquoy? Jenny wondered aloud. Had he maybe missed the fine smells of brown sugar, coffee, and apples in the yard where he had first appeared? 'No,' said Tom Strynd. 'Fankle hasn't come back here to live. I'm sorry, Jenny. I'll send you word if he does.'

Jenny thanked the merchant and turned away. It was getting dark. There was a star over the chimney. How would she ever find Fankle in the darkness?

'If you should ever want another kitten,' Tom Strynd called after her, 'I'll keep you in mind, supposing Silas Ingison ever dumps another one in the back of my van.

Jenny shook her head and moved on.

Mrs Martin, in the manse sitting-room, was very concerned to begin with. Had Fankle ever been gone so long before? Had Fankle been quite well recently, and lapped his milk and licked the fishbones clean? (She poured Jenny a tall glass of lemonade that she had made herself. Jenny sipped the lemonade gratefully; her throat was dry with grief and over-much speaking.) Mrs Martin smiled when Jenny told her about Ma Scad and her elegies. (Jenny took a big gulp of lemonade and felt more cheerful at once. She didn't know whether it was the lemonade or the kind old lady that made her feel better.) Mrs Martin declared that Fankle was the cleverest cat in the island — no, in Orkney — no, in the whole world. Wasn't it Fankle who had cured her of her trouble, with his antics in the garden that fine day? Fankle had unlocked in her the little spring that had lain hidden and dark for so long. ('Drink up, Jenny, there's plenty more lemonade. . . .') That cat was so wise he seemed to have known what ailed Mrs Martin. Did Jenny think for one moment that an extraordinarily intelligent cat like Fankle could vanish into thin air? Fankle was unique. Fankle would be home in the morning. (Jenny drained the lemonade glass to the last drop. She did like this wise old lady who had suffered so much.) They kissed at the door. The sky was thick with stars. Somewhere through the night, Jenny knew now, Fankle was moving, the essence of night and secrecy and wisdom.

Old Sam Swann the tailor was sitting beside his kitchen fire listening to the wireless when Jenny arrived. Old Mrs Swann sat at the other side of the fire, in a rocking chair, knitting a jersey.

'Have you seen my cat Fankle?' asked Jenny shyly. She had never been in this house before.

Behind the curtains was the tailor's bench, with its mingled smells of cloth, chalk, and resin.

Jenny had come here, on an impulse. Going home, she had suddenly remembered her father saying that Sam Swann the tailor was the greatest expert on cats in the island. There was nothing he didn't know about cats. People came from all over with their sick cats to the tailor shop, and more often than not Sam Swann knew the cure.

'Isn't the wireless a fine thing?' he said in his small sweet voice to Jenny. 'It tells you things. It educates you.'

He was a very eccentric man, Sam Swann. Though he knew everything about cats, he didn't keep a cat himself. If somebody whose cat he had cured asked him to name a fee, he would say something like, 'Oh yes, I think it *will* be a fine day tomorrow, indeed,' or 'General Amin seems to be stirring things up in Africa.'

'It's about my cat Fankle I've come,' said Jenny. 'He's been missing three days.'

'I don't know what I would do without the wireless now. I don't know what in the world Annabella would do. . . .' Annabella Swann, who was as deaf as a door-nail, knitted away steadily.

'Is it usual,' said Jenny, 'for cats to go away for three days at a time?'

'I'll tell you what I heard on the wireless tonight,' said Sam Swann. 'A talk about the planet Mars. I learned a few things. There's volcanoes and ice-caps on Mars. Fancy that.'

'I don't think Fankle's sick,' said Jenny. 'At least, he didn't look sick last time I saw him. But he might have suddenly got sick. Is this true, Mr Swann, that cats when they get sick go away and eat grass and get better that way?'

'Another talk last night,' said the old man, 'was about the American War of Independence. That was in George the Third's day, a long time ago. It all started with a gang of ruffians dumping chests of tea into the harbour at Boston, Massachusetts. There's never a day I live that I don't learn something from that wireless.'

'Goodnight, Mr Swann and Mrs Swann,' said Jenny.

Sam Swann followed Jenny to the door. 'All that music too on the wireless. High-class stuff, Scottish dance music. Tell me now, Jenny, do you *really* like that pop music?'

Outside, the night was as black as coal, or tar, or treacle.

Jenny didn't know whether to laugh or cry. The old man said in her ear, in the doorway, and winked, 'Cats sometimes fall in love, you know.'

Jenny was just going to bed when there was a loud double knock at the door. 'Who can it be,' said her father, 'at this time of night?'

It turned out to be Ma Scad. 'Is that girl, what's-her-name, Jenny, in?' she demanded. 'She was at my door earlier, asking about a black cat. Well, I have a message for her. A certain farmer in this island – I'm mentioning no names, I've been in trouble that way before – if you go, Jan Thomson, to a field of a certain farmer in this same island, you'll find a post in the middle of the field, and hanging down from the top of the post is *a black cat*. So I heard, not half-an-hour ago. I came here at once. A dead black cat, to scare the birds. Tell your girl that. I thought she might want to know.'

The very next morning Fankle turned up. He was tired and thin and hungry, but he had roses and moonlight in his eyes.

54

Revenge

The largest trout ever caught in the island was a twelve-pounder. That trout had been caught in the little island loch by a ne'er-do-well called Steve Smith, in the year 1924. Steve, who lived in a hovel on the loch shore, thought nothing about it at the time; only how he was to have little to eat but trout — fried trout, grilled trout, boiled trout, trout soup, trout and apples — for a whole week and more. The prospect depressed him, for he didn't like trout to eat all that much. He was very relieved when Mr Twamm, who owned the little hotel in the village, gave him a pound for the fish. Mr Twamm got the trout stuffed; had a suitable case made; and the largest trout ever caught in the island hung thereafter in the hall of the hotel, a proclamation and a challenge.

The island was visited every summer by a number of trout fishers, all of whom stayed in the hotel. They looked with envy and longing at the twelve-pound trout in the hall-way of the hotel. If only they could catch one half that size! One of them was heard to declare, over his malt whisky, that he would give his left hand to land a trout as large! But of course they were only joking. They knew they would go to their graves with nothing larger than a four-pounder to their credit. Indeed they were quite content, on a summer evening, to catch a couple of half-pounders; which they would hand in at the hotel kitchen, to be fried for breakfast next morning.

But there was one man in deadly earnest about breaking the record. Lieutenant-colonel Stick came every summer to the island, with his large fat wheezing wife, Mrs Stick, and his pretty, plump, earnest daughter Constantine. The colonel himself was as thin as a twig, which caused the islanders to say that he had been very aptly named. His neck was like a rope with a skin-clad skull on top of it. His knickerbockers cracked in the wind about his thin shanks, as he stood in the dinghy and fished, fished, fished from June to September. 'I'll catch a thirteen-pounder before I die,' he whined through his nose. 'I will. I will. I will.'

But all he caught were little tiddlers, or half-pounders, or pounders. One marvellous day he caught a six-and-a-half-pounder. His thin face split with delight as he weighed that trout on the hotel scales. Mrs Stick and Constantine were pleased that day, too — it meant that the vinegar of him would be changed to honey, for one evening at least. But then the colonel's eye caught the fish in the display case, and he scowled. Why should a tramp like Steve Smith have all the glory, while he, a gallant and honourable soldier, was condemned to fish, fish, fish, for little bits of tarnish? It was an unfair world.

Every evening that summer, as the colonel turned his back on the loch, he observed a black cat sitting on the

grassy verge above. This black cat knew a thing or two,
that much was obvious. As soon as a trout fisher waded
ashore, there was this black cat waiting for him. As often
as not the trout fisher would throw him a little fish, and
then Fankle — for of course it was Fankle — would begin
to devour it with the utmost greed and delicacy. The trout
fishers all grew to be fond of Fankle. They seemed to
think that Fankle, and his blackness, brought them luck.
(Fishermen are very superstitious.) Often they would
turn round, where they stood thigh-deep in the loch, to
see if that black cat was anywhere on the bank above. If
Fankle was there, washing his face or chasing a butterfly,
sure enough they would catch a decent fish within the
next half-hour. They all had the greatest regard for Fankle,
except Colonel Stick.

Colonel Stick waded ashore one day, tall and thin as a
heron, and all he had in his bag was a quarter-pounder and
a six-ouncer. The black cat approached, he coiled himself
sinuously, and with deep affection, around the rubber
ankles of Colonel Stick. The next thing Fankle knew, he
was struggling in cold brackish loch water! The colonel
had hurled him there, with one violent kick! There was not
a more wretched cat than Fankle when finally he struggled
ashore. He looked as if he had been dipped in a tub of
slime. He shivered. He sneezed. The three swans on the
loch looked at him with disdain.

Fankle dragged himself home, to be comforted and
dried and warmed and fed by his dear friend Jenny.

Sometimes Fankle would walk all the way to the hotel.
He was very popular in the hotel kitchen, where Annabel
the cook and Alfie the kitchen boy would treat him to all
the scraps from the plates of the rich over-fed trout fishers.

The first coolness of autumn was in the air — the island
oatfields were full of ripe secret golden whispers — when a
wonderful thing happened to Colonel Stick; he hooked the
largest trout he had ever seen! It happened in the middle

of the loch. On that particular afternoon Steve Smith, now
an old man with a brown wrinkled face, was acting as the
colonel's ghillie — that is, he was rowing the gallant gentleman here and there about the loch, and seeing to the gear,
and advising on this and that matter. 'You could do worse,'
Steve had said, 'than have a try over beside that little islet
with the ox-eye daisies growing on it. I saw two or three
big ones jumping there. . .' 'Very well, my man,' the
colonel had deigned to reply, 'row in that direction.' After
a couple of casts, a huge underwater obstacle disrupted the
splendid rhythm of the colonel's fishing. 'Damn it!' he
cried. 'Blast and damn! It's stuck in weed.' But then the
obstacle made a powerful swerve and lunge. 'Hold on to
it,' said Steve Smith. 'You've caught a big one.'

The colonel was so excited he nearly dropped the rod.
His Adam's apple wobbled in his throat. He did all the
wrong things, such as reeling in when he should have given
the fish more line. In fact he made such a mess of it that
in the end Steve Smith had to take the rod out of his hand.
When he felt the huge power on the hook, Steve whistled.
His own frail body responded with a surge of joy. Man
and fish fought with each other. After twenty minutes an
immense trout lay thrashing itself to death on the bottom-
boards of the dinghy. The colonel gaped at it in awe.

There was nothing to be done then but row ashore. The
colonel gave Steve Smith an extra fifty pence, over and
above his fee, for his help. He stuffed the speckled bronze-
and-silver-and-rose splendour into his bag; it was so huge
the head and the tail stuck out.

A certain black cat had observed the drama from the
door of the boat-shed.

The colonel's only concern now was that this treasure of
a trout should tip the scales at over twelve pounds. What if
it was eleven pounds eight ounces! The colonel thought of
cheating — of stuffing a sizeable stone into the trout's
maw. But immediately he regretted it. He was, after all,
an honourable man.

A little lithe black shadow flowed after the colonel, twenty yards behind, as the colonel strode on towards the hotel.

The monstrous fish was placed on the scales. The needle swung and hung and quivered upon twelve pounds four and a half ounces! The colonel wept with joy. He embraced his enormous lady. 'If I die tomorrow,' he half sang, 'I die a happy man!'

Guests and hotel workers gathered round this king of trout. They nodded. They smiled. They admired. (Privately, each was sorry it hadn't been caught by somebody else.)

Mr Twamm the hotelier came out of his office and congratulated the colonel.

'Take that down!' said the colonel, indicating the prize trout caught in 1924. 'Remove it. Let room be made for my champion!'

'What a fuss,' said his daughter, 'about a fish that nobody is going to eat!' (It wasn't that Constantine Stick was unromantic; she was genuinely and actively concerned for the poor and undernourished of this earth.)

The colonel frowned at Constantine. But then, his eye again lighting on his treasure, he summoned all present, even the kitchen boy, into the bar for a celebratory drink.

It cost him all of twenty pounds sterling, in ringing toasts and pledges. Alfie the kitchen boy drank too much beer and had to go out and be sick among the rhododendrons. When he returned to the bar he was still half-tiddly. He muttered something about 'a black cat whooping it up in the hall. . .' But nobody at any time paid any attention to Alfie. The colonel called for a last round — 'make it doubles this time' — whatever they wanted.

When the colonel stole out from the circles of drinkers to enjoy a private view of his heart's-desire, the fish was not exactly down to a skeleton. That would have been an impossibility, even for a cat of Fankle's voracity and bottomless stomach. But several large gashes had been trenched in the splendid flank. It was as if a knife had been taken to the *Laughing Cavalier*. Ravages of speckled skin, tatters of flesh.

It was Mrs Stick who heard the low moan from the hall, under the bar chatter and clink of glasses. She had heard it perhaps twice before in her life, when the colonel had been in extremis, once when his Rhodesian shares had crashed and another time when he got an abcess in his jaw.

She said to Constantine, 'Wait here.' She went out into the hall. She saw, beyond her hunched and broken husband, a black cat groaning with excess trout on top of the reception desk. Then the black cat looked over at the colonel, and it seemed, in spite of its sufferings, to smile.

Poetry and Prose

Fankle lay curled and seemingly asleep under Mr Tindall's desk, a thing which happened frequently, for as often as not he accompanied Jenny to school, like Mary's lamb.

'Now,' said Mr Tindall, 'are your pencils sharp? Start at a clean page in your jotters. Composition this morning.'

Most of the children groaned inwardly. Composition was not the favourite subject in that school.

'Dear me,' said Mr Tindall, 'we seem to have tackled about every subject on earth. I'm stuck for a subject. Any suggestions?'

Jimmy Riddack whispered, 'Fankle,' holding out a crumb of bread from his play-time piece. Fankle stirred, but slept on.

'Well, now, James,' said Mr Tindall, 'I think that's a

good idea. You will write an essay on Fankle the cat, a hundred words long. Begin.'

At the end of half an hour the pupils stood up one after the other and read their essays on Fankle aloud.

FANKELL THE THIEF

Fankell is a big thief, he stoll a chicken out off our press, he stoll Moira's blackbird, he stoll a pund of sossiges out of the van, he stoll butter from the hall kitchen, he stoll the kurnel's prize trout, I wonder sometimes if Fankell does any thing ells but steal.

(Barney Bell)

*

Fankl is Jenny's cat. Jenny is lucky. I wunce had a cat, her name was Tibb. Tibb was run over by the Glebe's tractor. Tibb was wanting to catch rats and rabbits when the Glebe's oatfield was being cut but instead Terry, the tractor man, ran over Tibb. I cried and I cried and I cried. This is all about Tibb but Tibb is not Fankl. Fankl is not so stupid as our Tibb. Fankl would not have let himself be run over.

(Agnes Gray)

*

F is for felicitous and funloving A is for astute N is for nocturnal K is for cunning (that is to say, if cunning were spelt with a "k") L is for legerdemain E is for errant, egregious, ecstatic, earnest, exquisite. All the above qualities and attributes, plus a thousand more, belong to the cat Fankle, of Inquoy in this island. But indeed all the 26 letters of the alphabet would have to be plundered to describe that cat, and still one would not have come anyway near the heart of the enigma that is Fankle.

(Robert Black)

*

One day I was out walking with my dad. My dad had his binoculars. My dad's hobby from being factor on the estate is nature study. My dad wants me to be a nature lover too, but I have always liked the creatures and the plants anyway. That day we saw an owl, a curlew, a kestrel, oyster-catchers, terns, and bonxies. And a hundred different kinds of wild flowers and many different wild animals (all of them I could and would write down only there's no space). Anyway, when we got home, my dad asked me what creature or plant I had liked best on that walk. I said Fankle, and he wasn't pleased about that. Fankle had been a shadow in the long grass.

(Alice Tweedale)

*

One day Fankle decided to be a man, not a cat. He bought trousers and a jersey and boots at the shop. He went home and wrote a letter to his cousin in New Zealand. He drank a glass of whisky at bedtime. He said, "Tomorrow I am going to the mart in Kirkwall to buy a cow and some sheep. . . ." Fankle was a rich farmer. He changed his name to Mister Frank Kelly. He got married. He had a girl and a boy. He had 2 tractors.

(Norman Fell)

*

Fankle is the name of my cat. I own Fankle, and Fankle owns me. He watches the crack in the flagstone. He hears things we can't hear, spiders spinning. I would like to be a lady or a powerful witch or a concert pianist in a long red gown at the Proms. I would like it if Fankle could tell me amazing stories out of his nine lives, going back long ages. I would like to be a poor girl who marries an emperor. But I am only Jenny of Inquoy, a croft girl, and Fankle is only a black stray cat I got from Mr Strynd. My mother says that's the way it is. Of course she is right. Fankle is the only cat that doesn't give my mother asthma. Mrs Martin of the Manse says she's sometimes sure Fankle is speaking to her. She loves Fankle. She gives Fankle tins of salmon or tuna on Fridays.

(Jenny Thomson)

*

Here is a poem I have made about Fankle.

FANKLE, *a poem*

There's a cat at Inquoy
Black as soot.
He eats fish.
He tries but he doesn't like jam or
    mustard or fruit.

Fankle belongs to Jenny,
Black as lampout,
Black as treacle,
Black as the forge when the blacksmith's
    away for the day,
Black as Africa.
He has eyes and claws bright as a breaking
    sea.

(Samuel Ingison)

*

Tam Black of Smedhurst is a coarse brute, everybody says. He won't let his wife wear rings or put scent behind her ears. Tam of Smedhurst *hates* cats. He kicks them. Yells at them. Puts his dog after them. Fires his shotgun at them. The day of the island show he tried to throw Fankle out of his yard. Now he has silver scars on his wrist.

(William Gray)

*

(All that Fred Kringle knew, after a hurried whispering session behind hands with Jenny, was that the cat's name began with "f". He wrote down a large black F near the centre of the page. After a while he drew a sailing ship flying a jolly roger in one corner. In the opposite corner he drew what might pass for a pyramid. He drew, with deep concentration, a long spiky flame-breathing creature — a dragon, possibly. He drew, and rubbed out, a motor van. Finally Fred drew a full moon with smiling eyes

64

like a Chinaman above the hill. . . .

This essay could not be read out. Mr Tindall pinned it — Fankle's heraldry — to the blackboard.)

*

Fankle slept all through this recital, but from time to time his ear twitched.

Snow

The snow came early that year. It came in the night, in great black whirls. It was still coming, at dawn, in great grey whirls. It was coming at noon, in great dazzling whirls.

When the children were let out of school at lunch time, their island was pure enchantment. Their island was all crystal and silver and swans-down. They ran into the snow, shrieking with joy. . . . They gathered snowballs; they pelted each other; they wept and laughed. Norman Fell got a snowball in his eye. Instead of scooping it out, like any other boy, he bawled as if he had been struck by an arrow, and he ran into the school to report Sammy Ingison for throwing the snowball at him.

Mr Tindall gave him a couple of sweets, and that silenced him. But when he came out to the ringing playground once more, the other children turned their backs on him.

Norman, with a snivel or two, turned and began to trudge home through the great folds of whiteness.

Which was purer and colder that afternoon, the snow or the children's laughter, it would be difficult to say.

Every time the boys and girls laughed or shouted, their breath made little ghosts in the air.

At last they stopped the chaotic snow-fight. They were exhausted. Their hair and jerseys and trousers were covered with white crumbs. Their cheeks shone like apples.

'What we'll do now,' said Sammy Ingison, 'is, we'll make a snowman!'

So, all twenty of them, aged between five and twelve, piled a snowman five feet high. They would have liked to make him ten feet high, or as high as the moon, but five feet was as high as they could manage. There he stood, a shapeless silver mass, only half-made, when Mr Tindall rang his bell for the resumption of classes.

'Norman, dear,' said his mother, 'what are you doing out of school? Is something the matter?'

The little blue-faced wretch, that was all the encouragement he needed. He burst into tears. Between sobs, he told how he had been deliberately hit in the eye by a snowball flung by Sammy Ingison.

'That Sammy Ingison!' cried Mrs Fell. 'A wicked boy he is, that's the truth! I'll have a word with his mother.'

'I was half-blind for a minute,' said Norman.

'No wonder, you poor dear,' said his mother. 'You're too delicate for rough games like that. Just wait till I get my hands on Sammy Ingison. Winter's not a good time for your health. You'll stay at home beside the fire, dear, and read books and listen to the wireless, till the snow's all gone. Yes, you will. I'll write a note this very afternoon and send it along to Mr Tindall.'

The blackest shape in the island that day flowed silently down the hill in the direction of Inquoy. Fankle hated snow much more than Norman Fell did. He lifted his delicate feet through the white cold alien stuff. He thought with joy of the fire at Inquoy, and a saucer of warm milk. Fankle would not have been out at all, on such a dreamlike morning; but he was interested in certain young hares he had recently noted on the hill. As a matter of fact, his journey had been fruitless. The hares — he might have known it — were snug in their burrows.

Fankle's way home led past the school. Would he go in? No, he needed that warm milk. Fankle saw that the children had piled a great mass of snow in the centre of the playground. It could have been anything — a white monster, a ruined crystal castle on the moon, a frozen ghost. Fankle considered it for a while. He disliked it, even though Jenny must have had a hand in it. He gave the half-made snowman a baleful glare, then he flowed on, a black snow-hindered shape, in the direction of Inquoy.

Twenty blackbirds sang along the telegraph lines, 'Look, we're the blackest things in the world, now the snow's here! There's no blackness in the world like ours! There isn't! We're intense blackness, thrilling blackness!'

Then they saw Fankle coursing home through the snow, and they stopped their boasting.

'I'll tell you what that boy is,' said Alistair Fell, 'he's a coward! You pet him, you mollycuddle him, you give way to every whim that takes him. I'm ashamed of that boy. He'll go to the school tomorrow. What would do Norman the world of good is a fight — a fist fight, with black eyes and bloody noses. Hit by a snowball, was he? Hit in his precious eye? By Sammy Ingison. What the precious darling should have done was take a fistful of snow and ram it down Sammy Ingison's jersey. And then ram another fistful between his teeth. The coward!'

Mrs Fell sighed over her knitting needles. She loved her husband almost as much as she loved her son. But he had that coarse brutal streak in him. He did not seem to understand how delicate the boy was. The poor little blue hands that he had brought home to her that afternoon — so sensitive and shivering. She was knitting a pair of mittens for him at this very moment. She wondered that those thin fingers didn't break off at first touch of the snow. She sighed again. Her knitting needles clacked.

'The well's frozen over,' said Alistair Fell. 'I'm going out now to break the ice.'

From the bedroom next door Mrs Fell could hear Norman playing his little matchbox-size transistor.

At home he was safe and happy. She smiled.

The school children could hardly pay attention to their lessons for thinking about the snowman. Mr Tindall had a hard time of it, trying to get them interested in the seven times table and the imports and exports of Norway.

When four o'clock came they almost broke each others' ribs to get out at the door.

They stood in a cluster round the half-made snowman. 'Of course he's like nothing on earth,' said Sammy Ingison. 'He hasn't got his uniform on, that's why. Now, we'll have to think about this very carefully.'

So the children laid their heads together around the naked creature from the purple clouds, and to each was assigned a duty. Such as:

From Mr Martin at the manse Jenny Thomson was instructed to ask for the loan of a black hat. It so happened that Mr Martin had a black broad-brimmed ecclesiastical hat, now turned somewhat brown and mouldy, that he had been thinking of putting in the fire. He had worn it in the first flush of his ordination. The hat was found; it was put into Jenny's hands by the plump kind hand of the minister. In due course it was placed, with reverence, on the snowman's head. It looked rather severe and clerical to begin with, but Sammy Ingison gave it a slight sideways tilt, and then the snowman suddenly acquired a rakish look.

It had been decided that lumps of coal would do for the eyes. The trouble was, all the houses in the island burned peats; all, that is, except the schoolhouse. Mr Tindall was tentatively approached. In no time at all two blue-black eyes stared out of the blank face.

A muffler, to keep the snowman warm — that was the next necessity. Jenny knew where a long muffler was, in the chest under the bed at Inquoy. She decided that she had better ask for it, although it was darned and moth-eaten and useless. It had belonged to her grandad, and he had worn it, sitting in the straw chair beside the fire, the winter before he died. She told her mother about the snowman, and how cold he would be that night under the stars. Her mother nodded. The long red-and-white scarf was brought from the chest; it had new moth holes here and there in it. But it was regarded by the children as a wonderful addition to the snowman's wardrobe. It was wound five times round his fat neck.

The snowman crackled with the first frost of sundown.

'An overcoat,' said Alice Tweeddale. 'Every snowman has an overcoat.'

Of course that was only an illusion. (Everybody knew that the snowman's overcoat was the thick quilting of snow itself.) But it added enormously to the illusion when Alice Tweeddale borrowed five red buttons from her grandmother. 'See you take them back here when the snow melts,' said the old woman. The five large red buttons were stuck all down the front of the snowman, in a line. He looked like a jolly fat man coming home from a party.

'Not without a pipe,' said Sammy. 'No snowman would be seen dead without his pipe.'

It was known that Barney Bell's father, the ferryman, smoked black twist in a pipe. 'He has two pipes,' said Barney. 'An old rank one, and a sweet-smoking one he got from mam for his birthday.' A pipe was brought from the ferryman's house through the star-shine, and stuck, upside-down, in the middle of the snowman's face.

There had never been a jollier presence in the island. His jollity infected the children. They laughed under the first stars, they danced around him, they kissed his overcoat, they showered each other with handfuls of snow. Tommy Wilson found a twig that became a walking-stick for him. The eyes of the children shone like stars under the glittering sky.

In the house at the jetty, Neil Bell the ferryman said to Isabel his wife, 'What's happened to it? Where's that pipe? I just don't understand it.'

'There it is, man,' said Isabel.

'Not that thing,' said the ferryman. 'That's pure poison. I'm looking for the pipe you gave me for my birthday, that tastes like honey. Where have you put it?'

'I never touched it,' said Mrs Bell. 'Barney was here after the school came out. He was wanting a pipe for a snowman or something.'

'It's a terrible thing,' said Neil Bell, 'when a man comes in cold from his work, and the thing he's most looking for, his pipe, isn't there. I'll warm that boy's ears!'

Neil Bell, tired though he was, walked the half-mile to the school. He met children, singly and in groups, drifting silently homewards through the purple and silver night. He did not see his own miscreant. When he got to the school yard, there the new king of the snow island stood, fatly and whitely gazing out over the fields and crofts, and the frozen wells and burns and waters. 'Sorry, man,' said Neil. He took his good pipe from the crackling mouth. 'See if you can do something with this other one,' said Neil. He put his putrid pipe where the sweet pipe had been (upside down, of course: all snowmen smoke their pipes upside down: Neil Bell remembered that from his boyhood). Then he turned and went home, for a decent smoke and a mug of sleepy ale.

When he did get home, Barney was prudently in bed.

*

There was an innocent at that school called Fred Kringle. Fred was more delighted with the snowman than any other child.

Fred got up very early on the third morning of the big snow. Not a single person in the island was astir. To the south-east the first light was spreading a flush over the snow. As Fred trudged schoolwards, he saw a diamond eye glittering in the window of Inquoy. Fankle at least was awake. Fankle was glaring disapproval at the snow. Fred couldn't understand why Fankle didn't like snow. Jenny had told him Fankle refused to go over the door-step. That first day had been enough for Fankle.

The snowman was, of course, in the school yard; he hadn't moved an inch. There was a new powdering of snow over one of his blue-black eyes, and a drift of snow in the rim of his hat; otherwise he was unchanged.

'Mister Snowman,' said Fred, 'here I am.'

The snowman acknowledged Fred in silence.

'Please come home and have breakfast in my house,' said Fred.

The snowman neither accepted nor declined the invitation.

'It's not good for you,' said Fred, 'standing out here in the cold, night after night. You'll get your death.'

A crystal of snow glittered on the snowman's cheek. The rim of the sun had risen over the neighbouring island. The church belfry stood black against the dawn.

'I tell you what you'll get,' said Fred. 'Porridge, and an egg — two if you like — and oatcakes and tea.'

The snowman seemed to take a long time thinking this out. He said nothing. A little flush came on his forehead.

'You're shy, that's what it is,' said Fred. 'You don't need to be shy. My mam'll make you feel at home right away.'

Still the snowman lingered.

'Come on,' said Fred. 'Please.' He put his small hand into the shapeless hand of the snowman. 'I'll walk with you all the way.'

Fred urged with his hand, gently, and the snowman's hand came off. In five or six fragments it broke and scattered. 'Oh, goodness,' whispered Fred. 'What have I done? I'll get into trouble for this, for sure. I wonder if I should get the doctor.'

But the snowman seemed to feel no pain or anger or resentment. Suddenly he took the risen sun full in the eyes. His face flashed.

Norman Fell was sick to death of books and wireless programmes and ludo. (What fun was there in playing ludo against yourself?) For three days he had listened, with envy, to the merriment drifting across the hillside from the school playground. He was sorry now he had told his mother about Sammy Ingison's snowball. He would certainly not get back to school till the last of the snow had melted; and by that time, of course, all the magic and fun would have melted into the light of common day.

Norman, before going to bed the previous evening, in the nest of hot water bottles his mother had prepared for him, had filled in a form which promised him, by return of post, a booklet that would let him into the secret of strength. He was promised thick shoulders and huge muscles. 'I will soon be the strongest boy in this island,' thought Norman, as he fixed the stamp on the envelope and licked down the flap. But he didn't want anybody to know about it.

He got up, therefore, when his mother and father were still abed. Stealthily he opened the outside door. A hinge squeaked like a little mouse, then all was silence again. It was a hundred yards from the farm to the red post box at the side of the road.

The snow crackled and snapped under Norman's feet. The island looked beautiful under the early sun. It looked like an island out of some fairy-tale. Norman thought how terrible it was that he should have missed all that, shut in his prison of a room (and all through his own stupid fault). Well, it would never happen again.

He stopped at the post box. He was about to drop the letter inside when his back, from neck to shoulder blades, was possessed by cold flames. The suddenness and shock took his breath away — he nearly fell among the snow.

There was a laugh behind him — a cruel contemptuous laugh — and at the same time more coals of ice were poured down inside his shirt. Sammy Ingison was saying "good morning" to Norman Fell in his own special way.

Norman turned and his clenched fist took Sammy on the forehead. Sammy was so surprised that his knees collapsed and he sat down on a snow hummock. Norman flung himself at the tormentor. He took him by the shoulders and pressed him down into the drift. Sammy's mouth was a red smoking O. Norman scooped up a handful of snow and stuffed it in. Sammy kicked him awkwardly and scrambled to his knees. He spat out his cold gag; while he was doing that Norman rammed two fistfuls inside his shirt. Sammy yelled with the thrilling pain of it, or else with the shock of being set upon by this gutless namby-pamby, mumma's little darling, who had now seized him by the lapels and was shaking him like a rat!

Sammy had had enough. It was more than a man could endure, especially before breakfast. He broke free, and ran. He turned at the end of the road. 'I'll get you for this, Fell,' he shrilled across the silver of the morning. 'You fudge that you are.'

When Norman got home his mother was stirring about the fire, getting the tea and the porridge made. She saw the flush on the boy's face, and the excited glitter in his eye. 'I've been out posting a letter,' he said. 'I fell in a drift. I got my shirt wet. But it doesn't matter. I feel very well this morning. I'm going to the school as soon as I've had my porridge.'

'Good lad,' said his father.

'Fankle dear,' said Jenny, 'what's wrong? You simply

must come and see our snowman. It's the loveliest snowman in the world.'

Fankle let on not to hear. He sat with his back to Jenny,
as if snowmen, snow-women, snow-children – all the
barren wintry breed – were a matter of supreme indifference to him.

'Goodbye, Fankle,' said Jenny. 'I must go to the school
now. Won't you walk with me down to the gate?'

Fankle did not so much as turn his head. He was obviously very displeased with his friend.

The snow remained, day after day, but after the fourth
day it no longer had its swan-plumage and crystal. Instead
it hardened and grew grey. The road became dangerous.
The ferryman Neil Bell slipped on it, coming up from the
pier, and broke his leg. The helicopter came, hovered over
the island, dropped down, hovered; and, huge insect of
mercy, drew Neil Bell into itself and bore him to the
hospital in Kirkwall.

Old Andrew Gray was never done telling the children
about the great snowfalls in his time. The snowfalls of the
last fifty years were poor things in comparison. Why, when
he was a boy, the loch in winter was a solid sheet of ice!
Farmers had driven horses and carts across it. Boys had
played football on it, night after night. This generation,
said old Andrew Gray scornfully, had only seen the
fringes of the loch frozen. But 'No,' said his grandson
Ollie, 'the loch's frozen across this winter. But we're
feared to go on the ice, in case it gives way.'

The old man snorted, and struck match after match
into his dead pipe.

That afternoon old Andrew Gray told his daughter he
was going out for a walk. Maurya told him to be careful,
the roads were very slippery. Old Andrew took his walking
stick in his hand and went out into the grey air. Instead of
keeping to the road, the old man crackled his way across
two fields to the loch shore. Across, on the other side,

lived Sander Black, his contemporary, whom he only saw
once a year, on the day of the agricultural show. They
were both getting very old. He was determined to pay
Sander a winter visit. It wasn't that he liked Sander Black
all that well, but more than likely Sander would have a
bottle of whisky in his cupboard, and he would get a dram
or two before dark. Old Andrew set out over the loch ice.
Once or twice he skidded and slithered here and there, but
he never lost his balance. At the centre of the loch the ice
broke under him, and old Andrew disappeared into a black
star of water. He would have died that day, only Sander
Black happened to be on the opposite shore of the loch,
stropping his appetite on a breath or two of frosty air. He
looked across the still grey loch, and he could hardly believe his eyes when he saw the small black figure approaching from the opposite shore. 'It's that old idiot,' said
Sander Black. (Sander had excellent eye-sight, for an old
man.) 'What does he think he's doing? He must be in his
dotage. I hope he isn't coming to visit me. I don't like him
all that well. Once a year, at the agricultural show, is
enough. . .' The old bent black figure on the ice came
nearer. There was a loud crack, like a rifle shot, and
Andrew Gray disappeared.

'What a way to die,' said Sander Black, wonderingly.
'There's worse ways, I suppose.' The public telephone box
was on the road-side, not twenty yards away. Sander
didn't like telephones or television, but he managed to tell
what he had seen to the hospital in Kirkwall. 'Not that it'll
do the poor old creature any good,' he said to the doctor
at the other end of the line. 'He's as stiff as a salt skate
by this time.'

The helicopter droned along the horizon. It hung over
the loch, dropped, went here and there. It drew up into
itself what was left of old Andrew Gray, a spark of life in
an ice cage. It went in a great slow arc in the direction of
Kirkwall and the hospital.

Three days later the old man was sitting up in bed and

smoking his pipe. 'I told them,' he said. 'I got tired of telling them. The snow and the ice nowadays are nothing like what they were when I was a boy. In them days you could have held the agricultural show on that loch, any day from December to February.'

It was dark when those who had gone to visit old Andrew in the hospital returned. As they passed Inquoy, going gingerly because of the increasingly dangerous road surface – all green and black ice – they saw two diamonds gleaming in the window.

Fankle was keeping ward and vigil.

The island, after six days, was sheathed in ice armour. The snowman in the schoolyard was no longer the jolly white flocculent teddy-bear of the first three days. There was a grimness about him. He began to look like a stout cruel knight arming himself for an unjust war. If a stone was thrown at him, he rang like iron. All at once, it seemed, the children turned away from him. They discovered an old sport that they had almost forgotten, so green the winters had been for five years past: sledging. Half-a-dozen sledges were unearthed from barns and outhouses. The nights sussurated and rang, and were lyrical with distant laughter, as the island children hurtled on their sledges down the slope of the hill.

'Fankle,' whispered Jenny on the second night of the sledges, 'I'm going out to sledge. You see, the snow will soon be gone, and then we won't be able to sledge for a whole year, maybe more. I'll see you when I come back. I'll warm some milk for you.'

Fankle paid no attention. There had never been such haughtiness or disdain in the croft of Inquoy. Fankle had fallen out with Jenny. He refused to acknowledge her presence. He sat gazing into the cheerful fire, and blinked now and then. He was his own cat. Let him be left alone. He could live quite happily by himself.

But he did not sit beside the fire all night. When the

rosy-faced children dragged their sledges home from the hill, there, at the croft window of Inquoy, twin diamonds blazed. Fankle was contemplating, for yet another night, the mystery of snow.

The snow vanished overnight. When the children were in bed — and they needed no stories or cocoa to make them sleep, those nights — the rain came, in sheets and torrents. For hour after black hour it rained, a warm persistent downpour. Every roof and window in the island drummed and throbbed — the gutters sang little songs all night — the pools along the road plashed.

When first light came, about eight o'clock in the morning, the island had shed its winter coat, except for a ragged patch or two of grey lace along the stone walls, and on the upper slope of the hill. And still the rain nagged and nagged at the last tissue of snow.

The children trooped, draggled, to school. The snowman had suffered a mighty defeat. He was a ruin, he was unrecognizable, he was a shrunken shapeless lump stuck about with buttons and pieces of coal and other items from the kingdom of man. Barney Bell took the pipe from the mess, shook it dry, and put it in his pocket.

'Perhaps,' said Mr Tindall the school-master, 'we'll be able to get some work done now.'

That night, Fankle decided to be friendly again. He condescended to speak. (Mr and Mrs Thomson were out, visiting their neighbours for an hour.) 'I won't deny it,' said Fankle. 'I was very hurt, Jenny. I would not have believed it — you, my best friend, deserting me for *a snowman*, a thing that's here today and gone tomorrow. Let me tell you this, Jenny, if that snow had gone on for a few days more, you wouldn't have had your Fankle. It would have been the end of me. You've no idea how much I suffered!'

'Poor Fankle,' said Jenny, and stroked him with all

the tenderness she had in her. 'Dear sweet Fankle!'

'Nasty white useless stuff,' said Fankle. 'Thank goodness it's gone. I can tell you, Jenny, I was very worried for a day or two.'

'What's so worrying about a snowfall?' said Jenny.

'Dear me,' said Fankle, 'human beings have short memories. I never cease being amazed. Perhaps you've never heard of the Ice Age.'

'Of course I have,' said Jenny. 'Thousands and thousands of years ago.'

Fankle licked his paw. He blinked at the peatflame. At last he turned sombre eyes on Jenny.

'There was more than one Ice Age,' he said, 'there were several. There will be another Ice Age sometime soon, when we least expect it. When I saw that first snowflake ten days ago I thought to myself, *This is it. Here it comes.* . . . But I said nothing. I didn't want to frighten you. I thought, *Poor innocent things, enjoying themselves on the edge of destruction, why should I disenchant them*?'

'You weren't a very good prophet of doom,' said Jenny, 'for the snow came and went like a million white blossoms, didn't it? It was very beautiful while it lasted.'

'Some winter,' said Fankle, 'the snow will come and it won't go away in a hurry. There'll be no springs or summers or autumns for ten thousand years. There'll be no silly children, either, dancing round an idiotic-looking white lump.'

Jenny let her imagination drift into that bleak awful time. She shivered, as if a first breath of it was on her flesh.

'The odds are,' said Fankle, 'you won't see it in your time, Jenny. Now that we're friends again, and have the house to ourselves, I'll tell you a story.'

'Goody gumdrops,' cried Jenny, and lifted Fankle in her arms, and rubbed her hair in the fur between his imperious ears.

'Put me down!' said Fankle. 'I refuse to tell the story, in such an undignified posture. . .'

Four-square on the rug again, Fankle said, 'There will be no snow in this story, I'm glad to say, except for a few silver scars on the mountain tops. Think of China. Think of an orphan girl beside the river, called Bat-ye, pulling reeds from the river bed. Think of the young lonely Emperor in his jade palace, the splendid rolling garden with grottos and fountains, green silk pavilions, a dragon's cave. I remember it all so well, Jenny. Are you listening?'

Poor River Girl

Bat-ye was a poor girl. Her father was a fisherman, but he was dead.

Bat-ye grew up to be tall and beautiful. Her hands were like flowers.

Bat-ye could say in a dry time, 'Cloud, be good to the earth.' And the rain would come; as it always does at last, anyway.

Bat-ye could say, when the floods rose, 'River, keep to your own house.' Then the poor people whose thresholds and goats had been drowned clapped their hands and laughed. (The waters would have gone down, sooner or later, whether Bat-ye had spoken to the elements or not.)

Bat-ye said, 'I am poor. Gold, come to my hands.' But Bat-ye remained poor and hungry, for three more years.

Then Bat-ye understood that a selfish wish was never answered; at least, not at once; and never in a way expected.

One day Bat-ye was pulling reeds from the river to make baskets. She sold baskets, and flowers, and little delicate grass cages with butterflies and grasshoppers in them, in the villages along the river shore. A man passed by on a horse, going along the river track. He said, 'Girl, you have beautiful hands.'

Bat-ye bowed her head.

The horseman said, 'I am the Emperor's Minister of Commerce. I live a thousand miles away, in a fine house just outside the capital. Last winter the old silk-weaver in my house died. My wife said, "When you are visiting the villages along the river, and the mountain villages, enquire after a good weaver of silk." I think I have found such a person.'

Bat-ye answered that she had never done such a thing as weave silk. She could only make baskets and grass cages.

'With such beautiful hands,' said the civil servant, 'you could weave silk better than anyone in the four kingdoms. Come.'

Bat-ye dropped her bundle of reeds. They floated down the river. She sat on the horse behind the Minister of Commerce. She saw soon that there were other horsemen, armed, riding behind. They shouted to each other, 'The minister has found a beautiful girl! . . .' 'This river girl is a better prize than all the taxes he has gathered from the delta. . . .' 'She is the sweetest thing our eyes have seen in ten thousand miles. . . .'

All the way to the capital, the great minister asked only one question, 'Girl, what is your name?'

She answered in such a low voice that it might have been two rain drops falling on a blade of grass: 'Bat-ye'.

'You will have a new name in my house,' said the Minister of Commerce. (Bat-ye means 'poor river girl'.)

At last they came to the minister's house. It had two court-yards, a fountain, twelve outside flights of stairs, a pet dragon in a cave, a wine-press, an orchestra of flutes, and a hundred servants.

Bat-ye was shown the looms, and the hanks of silk, and the breeding silkworms. She put her hands among the silk. Her hands were like swans fishing in bright water.

After a week, Bat-ye began to make beautiful silk.

The minister's wife decided that her new name should be 'Girl of Tulips'.

Girl of Tulips was lonely in the palace. She did not understand the language of the people — only a word here and there. She missed the fishing-folk. She missed the buyers and sellers at the river markets. She missed the cry of the water-bird.

She said, 'I am lonely. I long for a friend.'

The minister's wife would have been her friend. But she had been sick for a year. She lay on her bed all the time. Her cheeks were red patches. Her arms were sticks. Not the lightest daintiest food would remain in her stomach. One day Girl of Tulips poached a little fish that she found swimming in the garden pool. She prepared the fish with milk and a little wine. She brought it on a blue dish to the minister's wife. The minister's wife ate the meal and said, 'That was delicious food. It lies kindly on my stomach.'

Later she said, 'Your hands are kind, Girl of Tulips. Take the silver from my forehead. I am drowning in sweat.'

At midnight she said, 'You are my dear friend, Girl of Tulips.'

An hour after midnight the Minister of Commerce, two doctors, and seven women entered the room where the woman lay. They stood silent round her bed.

At dawn the minister's wife died. 'Close her eyes, Girl of Tulips,' said the minister.

The dead woman lay on her bed like a girl asleep under a tree.

The seven women put on black masks. They danced slowly.

Then grief broke out throughout the palace, like floods and like tempest and like thunder. The cook wept into her pot of soup.

Girl of Tulips did not weep. She had got the friend she asked for, but only for an hour.

Beautiful sheets of silk, beautiful rolls of silk, issued from the looms. The hands of the girl went serenely among the silk like swans on a brimming river.

One night she wept: 'I have no one I can love. Alas!'

The very next morning she felt against her leg, while she sat at the loom, a stroke and a brush of exquisite softness. She thought for a moment that life had entered one of the hanks of silk. She looked down. A small black cat was rubbing against her shin-bone. It was the loveliest kitten she had ever seen. 'You will stay with me in my room, black cat,' said Girl of Tulips. 'You will have milk of unicorns to drink. You will have peacocks' brains to eat. You will sleep on a drift of flower petals.' (That was imagination and poetry, of course. All she could give the kitten was bits of half-chewed chicken and ordinary milk.)

At the end of the funeral, the shimmering body fell through its great cage of flames. The flames leapt higher, roared louder. When at last the pyre was all ashes, multitudinous grey whisperings, in the emerald casket at the heart of the pyre was a strewment of finer ashes. The dust of the woman was given to the four winds.

Household voices cried, 'Farewell, dear lady. . . .' 'Go joyfully into the House of the Elements. . . .' 'Your pleasant deeds and words are with us always.'

Girl of Tulips said, 'Go, friend.'

When she looked up, she saw that the Minister of Commerce, the widower, her lord and master, was standing before her. He looked at her for a butterfly-time with sad, beseeching eyes.

Her eyes were in the dust.
He left her alone in the garden.

Girl of Tulips said, idly, 'I have lost a friend. Do you hear that, cat? I don't know what name to give you, cat. Cat, I need love in this poor life of mine. Let love come, soon. Cat, the lord of this house loves me, but I do not love him. Love is cruel and sweet. Perhaps my lord will send me back to the river when he knows for sure that I cannot love him. I will be poor again. I will marry a fisherman and gut fish. Cat, you have the wisest look I have ever seen on a creature. Perhaps I will call you Midnight. Cat, I am sick with longing.'

The minister did not send his silk-weaver back to the river. Instead, he contrived in every way to make life richer for her. He gave her the most beautiful room in the house, looking towards the mountain with silver scars at its summit. Every morning a box of delicious confectionery was brought to the weaving shop by a servant. She was given two servants who attended to all her needs and wants. They robed and disrobed her. They handed her down the steps into her bath of perfumed water. They surrounded her with flowers. Musicians played while she slept. They would have fed her from golden plates if she had let them.

Occasionally, on one of the flights of stairs, or in the garden, Girl of Tulips and the minister would come face to face. One cold face, one face that was a looking-glass of joy, confusion, beseeching, pain, hopelessness.

Every time, Girl of Tulips shook her head.

The minister would bow, turn, and go about his business.

Then, at her ankle, the caress of black silk. The cat with no name was never far from his mistress.

It could not go on for ever, that strange wooing. One morning Girl of Tulips came into the weaving chamber. She found red words pinned to the loom. 'The lord the

Minister of Commerce requests of Girl of Tulips the happy
and well-handed mistress of the looms (once a poor river
girl) that she become his lady and the mistress of all this
broad and beauteous and fruitful estate. I have written
this with the blood of my heart. Answer soon. Answer
sweetly.'

'Love is cruel,' said Girl of Tulips to her cat. She wept.
Then she seized a piece of charcoal and wrote NO in large
reckless letters across the page. She went out into the
garden then. She did not cry any more. She sat still, with
the black cat in her lap, cold as a statue.

She did not sit for long. Three men from the minister's
bodyguard approached through the flowers. They had
ropes in their hands. They seized her without a word.

I forgot to say that the minister had, on his estate, apart
from the flutes, the dragon grotto, fountain, and wine-
press, an underground dungeon. There, in the blackness,
Girl of Tulips was immured. The walls dripped dampness.
Occasionally a chain rattled in the distance. She would be
wakened from her sleep by a thin lost shriek.

Her only comfort was the little black engine of delight
that trembled upon her bosom.

Time had no meaning in that dungeon. What did her un-
loved lover mean to do with her? She thought, after a
seventh pang of hunger had gone through her, that he must
have sentenced her to death by starvation.

A rat stirred in the corner of her cell. She cried out in
terror. The black cat flowed from her shoulder, and the
rat withdrew into its hole.

The terrible place intruded into her dreams. A white
shape lay stretched on the floor, bound and staked. A
figure in a dark robe bent over the helpless one. 'Love!'
it commanded. 'Love! Love!' 'No,' whispered the victim.
The torturer nodded. Half-naked men with torches and
knives approached. Their faces were blank. . . .

When Girl of Tulips woke, sweating, from that dream,
the sweetest moment she had ever experienced was the

song of the black cat on her breast, and his eyes like diamonds in the gloom.

Before she dropped off to sleep again, she heard a pro-
longed thrilling echo. A fanfare of silver trumpets was
being sounded from the gate above. There was a muted
pulse of drums. Some great event was about to happen.

Girl of Tulips whispered, 'What is love? . . . .' Then she
was folded softly, in the poppy of sleep.

The Emperor had arrived. That was the reason for the
ceremonial music at the gate. The Emperor and his retinue
had arrived, having given only an hour's notice. The
Emperor had decided to make a leisurely progress through
his four kingdoms. At every great house, beginning with
his Minister of Commerce, he would have to be expensively
entertained.

The banquet was spread in the great hall, overlooking
the garden.

The Emperor sat at the head of the table, the Minister
of Commerce sat at the foot. A hundred lords and ladies
ate and drank. Stylish words were spoken across the table.
It was as if an intricate web of wit and delight was being
woven.

In the middle of the third course — young eaglets soused
in strawberry wine — grains of spice got into the Emperor's
nostril. He sniffed, he grew rigid, there was no breath left
in the royal nasal passages for a full half-minute. The idle
elegant chatter around the board ceased. Mouths gaped.
The minister made agitated signs to one of the flunkeys.
The flunkey picked up a silk napkin from the sideboard
and rushed with it to the Emperor and thrust it into his
hand. It was not a moment too soon. The Emperor's head
shattered, twice. His royal nose exploded into the silk
napkin.

Then all around the light laughter and chatter broke out
again. The minister called on the musicians to play a piece
of music to unleash the digestive juices.

'You keep pungent spices in your kitchen,' said General Wo, the Emperor's aide-de-camp.

Little fountains of laughter leapt up here and there around the table. The next course, pears and apricots chilled in mountain ice, was announced.

Why was the Emperor so preoccupied? Ever since his sneezes, he had been gazing at the crumpled silk in his hand.

He said at last, 'How comes it, minister, that you have a better silk-weaver in your house here than I have in the Imperial Palace?'

'It is a matter of chance, your majesty,' said the minister.

'I have never handled silk like this,' said the Emperor, 'of such purity and softness, of such incomparable artistry. What is the name of your silk-weaver?'

'She is called Girl of Tulips,' said the Minister of Commerce, and bit his lip.

'I wish to see this silk-weaver,' said the Emperor.

'Alas,' said the minister, 'Girl of Tulips is not here. Girl of Tulips has been sent away. Girl of Tulips has woven her last silk.'

The Emperor drew his brows together. It was as if a thundercloud had settled there.

'Where is she?' he said. 'Tell me where this girl is. I will send out horsemen. She must be brought here as soon as possible. I delight in fine silk.'

The Minister of Commerce began to stammer. 'Majesty. . . . The truth is. . . . This Girl of Tulips is a very common person. Her true name is Bat-ye, which means "poor river girl". . . . That is exactly what this person is. When I first saw her she was in rags, she was smelling of brine. . . . She is nothing. . . . I would not have your eyes insulted. . . . Her behaviour is as common as her appearance. . . . She is ignorant, impudent. . . . For certain things she did recently here in this house, I got rid of her. . . . Think no more of Bat-ye, that common slut, your majesty.'

The musicians hung breathless upon their flutes.

'I want the girl for my looms,' said the Emperor at last. 'Minister, you will produce the girl, wherever she is, within a week. Otherwise, there will be a certain rearrangement of personnel within my council of state.'

The household had never seen such woe-begone looks on the face of their master — not even on the morning of his wife's death.

At last he crooked a finger at the chief flunkey, and whispered in his ear. He pointed downwards, through the floor, into the darkness under the foundation stone.

The next course was announced: sharks' fins and honey sauce. The minister ate nothing.

Girl of Tulips was free! There was a sudden torrent of light and fresh air into her cell. At first she thought they had come to summon her to the stake.

It was not the ferocious guards. It was her two hand-maidens who stood, smiling, on each side of the door. They drew her along a corridor that rang like an evil bell, and up iron stairs smelling of rust and pain and blood, and out at last into the garden. (The garden was a miracle of light and leaf, bee and shadow, blossom and scent, to the freed girl.) She was not allowed to linger in the garden. She was taken inside, the clothes smelling of earth-damp were stripped from her, she was laid languorously in a warm fragrant bath. Then the fine clothes she had worn before her imprisonment were, newly laundered, arrayed on her.

'What is happening?' said Girl of Tulips. 'Where will you take me now?'

The handmaidens could not say. They touched their fingers to their lips. They kissed her. They put delicate smiles on her.

Upstairs, downstairs, through a long corridor with music at the end of it, a confusion of voices, and such aromas of food that it was like an emerald sword entering her stomach. (She had not eaten for three days.)

She saw, seated at the long table, all the beauty and

valour of the region. At the far end, like a man sentenced, slumped the Minister of Commerce.

A stranger more splendid than any peacock rose to his feet as she entered. A single trumpet was sounded.

'Kneel,' whispered one of the handmaidens. She went down on her knees. How was she to know who he was? He was so handsome and richly attired he could have been one of the gods from the snow mountain.

He spoke. She dared to take her eyes from the floor. Her heart thumped erratically. He had the kindest, sweetest face she had ever seen on a man. If he had been a brine-smelling fisherman from the delta, with such a face she would have loved him. . . . His words, till now, had been only a confused music in her ears. She strove to understand; '. . . command you therefore, Girl of Tulips, to return with us at once to the Imperial Palace. The sight of you pleases us. A place will be found for you, suitable to your beauty and talents.'

'Speak to the Emperor,' whispered one of the handmaidens. 'Answer.'

'Of course I'll go with you,' said the honest girl from the river. 'But not because you're an emperor and can give me whatever I desire. No. I will go with you because I love you.'

She said these last words with her eyes on the ground.

The Emperor was suddenly kneeling beside her. He took her by the hands. He whispered, so that only she could hear, 'It is not only the silk. I would love you, Girl of Tulips, if you patched rags in a garret.'

Then he kissed her.

All the guests shouted and clapped their hands. They drowned the music of the flutes. The ladies laughed falsely. 'All happiness to your majesty!' shouted the guests. 'Happiness — prosperity — peace.'

The Minister of Commerce, at the foot of the table, buried his face in his hands.

The Emperor raised Girl of Tulips to her feet. He

kissed her fingers that still smelt faintly of rust and earth-mould.

In the heart of all that pageantry and excitement, a small black cat strolled nonchalantly under the table, and began to devour the scraps and fragments of food that had fallen from the feast. (Remember, he had not eaten for three long days.) Afterwards he gave his face a lick, yawned, and curled up at the entangled feet of his new master and mistress.

Before he dropped off to sleep, the black cat heard the Emperor say sternly, 'As for you, Minister of Commerce, my impulse is to have you executed at once. Impalement, disembowelling – a death like that seems suitable. She who is to be Empress has spoken on your behalf. You have suffered much, she says, and most of the time you are a just man. She has mentioned a fragrant ghost, your wife. You will therefore be left in peace. Let this be sufficient punishment – the knowledge that once you came within a few days of starving the future Empress to death'.

So it happened. The Emperor and Girl of Tulips were married with great state in the Imperial Palace. The celebrations went on for a month. The fisher people of the river heard at last that there was a new Empress, but they did not know that it was their friend Bat-ye.

The last dead firework lay in the imperial garden, one summer dawn.

It was time for the Emperor to return to his arduous duties.

Arduous they were – far more difficult than the tasks of a fisherman beside the river, or a fowler, or a hunter of tigers, or a silk weaver.

One morning, a month after the wedding, the Emperor came into his wife's chamber, after a council-of-state meeting, wringing his hands.

'A whole fleet of merchant ships!' he cried. 'Scattered in a storm! Half of them sunk. It was a very precious cargo, tea and jade and spices! Two merchants in the sea-port will be ruined!'

The Empress stroked her black cat, and said nothing.

The Emperor went out again. Who expects advice from a woman? He went to consult this maritime adviser and that.

The black cat stopped purring. It spoke to the Empress for the first time. It laid its head on her shoulder and whispered things into her ear.

When the Emperor returned to his wife's chamber, for a glass of tea and a few consoling kisses, she said, 'I wouldn't worry about the merchants so much. They're well insured against storm and shipwreck. They make a hundred times more than they ever lose. There will be sailors' widows now in all the little villages along the coast. Winter is coming on. See that the women and the children are all right. They are the ones who really suffer, after a disaster like this.'

The Emperor looked at the Empress with astonishment. He had never looked at the situation from this particular angle.

'I think there's truth in what you say,' he said.

The black cat slept, or pretended to sleep, on his favourite stool that was patterned with flowers and peacocks.

That weekend the families of the drowned sailors were given silver and an imperial guarantee of food and shelter until the following spring. The great merchants grumbled and said it could not be afforded. But they were not noticeably poorer themselves.

Five or six weeks later the Emperor came into his wife's chamber clasping his head in both hands. The council of state had just finished an emergency sitting. 'Terrible!' he cried. 'A revolt! My own people, that I love dearly, to take up swords and catapults against me! They will suffer for this. There will be heads rotting in the wind along a hundred miles of mountain road. Those gentle people from the mountains – goatherds, falconers, timber-men — who would have thought they would rise against their Emperor!'

The Empress stroked the black cat and was silent.

The Emperor went out, to consult a few generals. What does a woman, however beautiful and good, know about treason and force of arms?

The black cat murmured certain words into the ear of his friend.

When the Emperor returned, to forget his worries for a while in his wife's arms, she pushed him away, gently, and said, 'There are no finer people than the mountain tribes. No people have shown you more loyalty and love. But people will do desperate things when they have a dragon for a governor. If I were you, I would make enquiries — urgent enquiries — into the character and behaviour of the mountain governor. He is an evil man. Examine the account books. Of every six trees felled on the mountain, the governor takes four for himself and one for you. It's the same with the falconers and the goatherds. The governor has set up a flogging post in every village. The fine house of the governor is teeming with slaves — girls that were, until last year, the happy daughters of the mountain-men.'

The Emperor looked long into the indignant eyes of his wife. Then he went out of the room.

The black cat stretched himself on the silken stool.

Next morning the wicked governor, who had of course returned to the capital at the first stirring of revolt, was executed in the city square. An embassy, carrying a cage of doves, was sent into the mountains. Words were spoken across a torrent. That night the mountain rang with joy and loyalty.

More than a year later the Emperor entered his wife's chamber; a star of astonishment had exploded across his forehead.

'Barbarians!' he said. 'Out of the west, in the strangest ship you ever saw! How can such a ship sail at all? It is so clumsy it should sink. But it has come ten thousand miles. Such ugly men too. Their faces are as lumpy and white as dough. The gods only know what kind of gibberish they speak. Their eyes are blue as ice, and they stick out. They walk like bears. They showed me what passes for a book with them. Queer, incomprehensible letters, and the pictures crude and garish — nothing like the work of our artists, with their delicacy and endless suggestiveness. I think we cannot have such creatures in our land. I never saw such naked greed on faces — it frightened me! — when they stared at our golden statues and fountains. Obviously they want to trade with us, across thousands of miles of sea and desert. How their greedy eyes opened wide when the bales of silk were spread out before them! We don't need, or desire, the produce of barbarians. I think the best thing to do, in the circumstances, is cut off their ugly ears and tell them to turn round and go.'

The black cat cried out once.

'That cat of yours startled me then,' said the Emperor. 'It was like a cry of warning.'

'Listen carefully, my dear,' said the Empress. 'This is the gravest moment of your entire reign. I agree with you. Send these men back the way they came. Here our government and our way of life are exquisitely balanced. It is attuned to the mountains and seas and stars and grains of dust that have shaped and nourished our people for thousands of years. Now the stranger has his foot among us. This is no isolated coming. He is the first of thousands and tens of thousands. They will overthrow everything that we hold to be precious and good. Give them a gift, to show that we entertain no evil against them, then let them go.'

The black cat was stalking from wall to wall in a very agitated manner.

'Of course you are right, as always,' said the Emperor. 'The Europeans will be sent away at once.'

'It is not so simple as that, alas,' said the Empress. 'We like to think that we are alone under heaven, a great and powerful and wise people, very favoured by the gods. But there are other peoples. We have seen a brown man from India and a black thick-browed man from the islands in the south. They have their own wisdom, which is different from ours, but equally precious to them. There are thousands of such nations over the broad rich cloth of earth and sea. Can we shut our gates against them for ever? We cannot. We are all children of the sun. It is our nature to seek each other out. It is desirable that we seek each other out, and try to understand each other. It could be that in the end, in this way, all the world will be one. Think of the richness and happiness and peace then, when all the diverse cultures of the world meet and mingle! Then we will be that much nearer the serenity and wisdom that the gods desire for us. Bid the strangers come in. Accept their gifts. Prepare rooms for them. It may be the greatest day of your entire reign.'

The black cat huddled, a shape of misery, in the furthest corner of the room.

The Emperor went out to see to the silver trumpets of reception.

The Europeans stayed for many years in the houses that the Emperor gave them. The people in time got used to their ugliness and uncouthness; also to the graceless inquisitiveness with which they pried into every object and circumstance. They had hardly more knowledge of ceremony than baboons. They wanted to experience everything at once, like ignorant children in a cake shop.

Suddenly one morning they said they wanted now to return home. They were growing old, they said. They wished to die in peace in their own lands.

Gravely, and with many gifts, they were bidden farewell.

'That's the last of them,' said the Emperor. 'I got rather to like them in the end, in spite of all their barbarous ways. You see, my dear, it wasn't really important at all, the coming of the Europeans. It neither helped us nor harmed us. It simply stirred our curiosity a little.

They won't come again.'

The Empress sighed. The black cat growled in her lap.

They grew old together, the Imperial pair. Never had the Empire known such happiness and prosperity. 'The gods bless our wise Emperor and Empress!' the people sang outside the gate on each anniversary of their wedding.

Troubles and difficulties came, of course. Whenever he was distracted by the jargon and vacillation and sheer stupidity of his council, the Emperor brought his beating pulses and flushed face to his wife's chamber; and there, into that wise and patient ear, he poured everything. Then, when he came back an hour or so later, she had the cure ready — the only possible solution in the circumstances.

And always the black cat lay curled on his patterned silk stool, as if nothing mattered in the world.

One day, when the Emperor was fishing in the artificial lake in the high garden, the Empress gave secret orders to the chief ostler. Within an hour a very plain-looking coach was standing at the main gate, harnessed to a pair of strong horses, one black and one white. When at last the Empress climbed aboard the coach, she was very plainly clad, almost as if she was the wife of the tenth secretary's under-clerk. The black cat cried out of a bamboo basket. The Empress whispered orders into the coachman's ear; then she put a map into his hand.

With a cry and a whip-crack the carriage moved off.

The Emperor dozed at the lake-side and was aware of nothing. (When he went in for his supper, of course, he found a letter under his plate on the table.)

That coach-journey lasted a full week. The horses had to be changed at this staging-post and that. The black cat *hated* travelling of all kinds. He complained often out of his bamboo prison. The Empress often bent down and whispered loving words through the bars.

Night after night they stayed at ordinary inns, where

sometimes they were received courteously and sometimes with indifference and coldness. At the hospitable inns the black cat always obliged by catching the rat that was the bane of the cook's life.

On the seventh day, at noon, the Empress began to take a great interest in her surroundings. 'That little hill with the one tree,' she cried, 'I remember it.' Then, later, 'The pool in the river where the children bathed — how beautiful. There's a boy wading in it now!' She tapped the coachman on the shoulder with her fan. 'Turn left at the first cross-roads. A village is down there, along the river bank.'

The coach stopped in the village square. The Empress got out. The black cat trotted at her heels. The coachman sat in the coach and chewed leaves. He thought, 'What a poor uninteresting place!'

All the men and women of the village were fishing that day, out of sight behind the river-bend. Only old villagers were left, sitting at their doorsteps in the sun. The children were playing along the river bank, sailing paper boats, bathing, fishing tiddlers with jars. The old men and women looked up, bright-eyed, at the stranger.

The black cat strolled down to the splashing, laughing, weeping, echoing river bank.

An old woman said, 'You're too early. If you want to buy a fish come back at sunset. The boats won't be home till sunset.'

The Empress said that she would like to buy a fish. She was sorry she was too early. Perhaps she could wait.

'What's your man, a scrivener?' said the old woman whose hand was like a bird's claw. 'Prosperous ladies like you don't usually come down to the fish market. They send one of their hoity-toity servants.'

The Empress said the village and the river were so beautiful, she was glad she had come.

All the old ones of the village laughed, some like frogs, some like reeds, some like gurgling water.

'Oh dear,' said the old woman, wiping her eyes on the

back of her hand. 'That's the first time anybody has said *that*! Beautiful, indeed — what could be more plain and ordinary than this village?'

An old man wheezed, 'You're a strange person, right enough. But there's something familiar about you, I can't just put my finger on it. . . .'

Down at the river-shore, all was suddenly silent. The children were gathered round the black cat, some kneeling, some crouching, some dancing on one foot.

The Empress said, 'Are the people of this village happy? Apart from a bad fishing season now and then, are they contented?'

She was answered by a chorus of cries, so confused that she could make nothing of it; all she knew was that it was a harsh music. . . . At last the old woman spoke for everyone.

'Happy?' she shrilled in her thin cracked voice. 'We old ones happy? Who cares about us? Nobody. We can't work any longer. We're useless. When the young ones come in with their baskets of fish, they might throw us a head or a tail. Well, we don't blame them. They must do the work, they must keep the village going. They have to eat and be strong. But, lady, everybody here would be well content if it wasn't for the officials and the tax-collectors. They come in their boats twice a year and they bleed us dry. They knock at every door with their parchments and purses. And all to keep the Emperor and his slut of a wife in luxury, somewhere far in the north. *They* don't have to worry. Their silks and goblets of wine and harps make old age pleasant for them. . . . But even so, stranger, it might be a happy village, imperial taxes or not, if it weren't for the war-lords who come and go with their armed bandits, leaving ruin and smoking houses behind them. This is happening all over the land. It happened here six years ago. Lady, why are you crying? This has nothing to do with you.'

The children at the river-bank were all suddenly looking

up at the steps where the Empress and the old village ones were holding their dialogue.

The Empress couldn't speak for a long time. She covered her face with her hands. But the tears oozed out between her fingers.

The old man said, 'She's the strangest lady I ever came across. And yet, I don't know, there's something about her. Her voice — she has the river-sounds in her voice. She doesn't come from some posh quarter of the city, that's sure.'

The Empress said, 'I think I don't have time to wait for the fishing-boats. But I'd like to buy something in the village. Have you any of your little grass cages for sale, where people used to keep butterflies and grasshoppers?'

The old villagers shook their heads.

The old woman said, 'No grass cages have been made here for a long long time. There was only one person who could make them properly anyway, and her name was Bat-ye. After Bat-ye died, there were no more beautiful grass cages.'

The eyes of a few old men shone like boys' eyes. One old man said, 'Bat-ye. Bat-ye was the sweetest girl who ever lived in this village. I loved Bat-ye. I can say it now. My old woman died last winter.'

'Bat-ye was more beautiful than any flower,' said another old man. 'Her hands were like lotus-blossoms.'

A third old man said, 'We might have known we couldn't keep Bat-ye. She was too rare and beautiful for a poor village like this.'

'What happened to Bat-ye in the end?' said the Empress.

'She was drowned one day in the river,' said the old woman. 'She was reaching down for a strong reed when the water covered her face. The river floated her out to sea. Her body was never found.'

'Not a day has passed,' said an old man, 'that I haven't thought of the beautiful hands of Bat-ye.'

'No, she wasn't drowned,' said another old man. 'The

bandits took her away to their cave in the mountains. A peasant saw her being forced on to a horse's back, bound and weeping. I shudder to think what those wicked men did to our Bat-ye.'

'I think,' said the old woman, 'the truth is simpler. Bat-ye got tired of this poor place. One day she left everything and went away to the city. I'd have done the same but I hadn't the courage. What Bat-ye did in the city I don't know. Someone like her might have opened a prosperous silk shop. I expect she's dead now. She never came back to the river, at all events, and I don't blame her.'

The children, the black cat among them, were coming through the reeds and the rocks towards the village. The children had eyes only for the strange woman standing at the steps. The eyes of the children were round, as though they had heard a wonderful fairy-tale. Two of the children were lustrous from the river water.

'Bat-ye, Bat-ye,' said an old man, and smiled like a boy.

'That's what happens to the poor river people,' said the old woman. 'They're hungry most of the time, they grow old, the salt of taxation is rubbed again and again into their sores. If a villager chances to be beautiful she is either dragged away, or she goes of her own accord to the city to better herself.'

The children stood around the group of old ones in a wide ring. 'The Empress,' breathed a little boy. 'Why is she not wearing gold and ivory?' 'The Empress,' said a girl whose hand was full of river-flowers.

'So, stranger,' said the old woman, 'we can't oblige you today, either in the way of a tasty fish or a grass cage for butterflies. Thank you, all the same, for stirring up such fragrant memories in us. Our hearts have been dead stems for a good few winters past.'

The old ones smiled all around the Empress.

The children murmured, 'Empress'. . . 'Empress'. . . A boy blew melodious air out of a reed.

'Get back to the river, you children!' cried an old man.

'This lady is nothing to you. Stop that whispering. I'll tell your fathers when they come back with the fish at sunset.'

The children only came closer.

The river gleamed between the reeds. Far off, fishermen called to hidden fishermen round the river-bend.

The Empress took a purse out of her bag. She said, 'This is the happiest day, almost, of my life. I would like to give you something in memory of it, so that you won't be poor again until you die. I remember all your faces, though time has put beautiful traceries on each one.'

The old villagers were quite bewildered by this speech. They had never seen gold coins before; that bewildered them further; what bewildered them most of all was that the stranger, as she laid a large gold coin in each withered palm, murmured gently the name of the recipient: 'Green-Fin'. . . 'Tide-Sparkle'. . . 'Silver-Scale'. . . 'Hook-in-the-Gut'. . . She was putting an Imperial guinea in the hand of the smiling old man, and trying to remember his name, when he seized her fingers and cried, 'Bat-ye! I think of the hand of Bat-ye every day. I would know Bat-ye's hand anywhere! Friends, our Bat-ye has come back to us!'

But what the children chanted, through strands of reed-music, was 'Empress!' 'Empress!' 'Empress!'

'She doesn't *look* like the Empress,' said the smallest boy. 'She looks just like the salt-merchant's wife, in that grey coat.'

'Bat-ye'. . . 'Empress'. . . 'Bat-ye'. The fresh voices and the withered voices mingled under the sun, with notes of music.

'It's a wonderful day,' said another boy, who had been bathing. 'A cat has told us a story. The Empress of the four kingdoms has come to visit our village.'

The mouths of the old ones were clustered like bees about the gold-shadowed fingers of the lady who had once plucked river-reeds. Their eyes brimmed with love and wonderment and remembrance.

The girl whose hands were full of blossoms went up to

the Empress and threw them over her. Petals clung to her coat, the scent of water-lilies drifted about her.

'My dear, dear friends,' said Bat-ye.

The children were still dancing round their guest when the first river boat returned, a lantern in her stern.

On the verge of the river a black cat yearned towards the smell of new-caught fish.

Moon Animals

An old lady is busy in her house. She seems to be expecting visitors.

She has been baking. The room is full of good smells. A tray of little cakes — cheese cakes, pancakes, rock cakes — smokes fragrantly on the sideboard.

She has been *very* busy. One or two patches of her flagstone floor are still damp from the washing.

Now she is putting wild roses in a vase in the window where a bluebottle sings and bumps.

Important visitors they must be.

A small airplane flies overhead. The old lady goes to her open door. She looks up, shading her eyes against the sun. She waves her hand, cries a welcome. Her visitors are in the plane.

They have come, three shouting children, two boys and a girl. They come out of the taxi, burdened with cases, duffle bags, coats.

'Grandma!' they shout. 'Thanks,' they shout. 'We're here!' they shout.

The old lady enfolds them, one after the other. She has many smiles, but no words yet. 'I'm Sam. That's Roger.' 'And I'm Margaret.'

'Grandma, we've got presents for you.'

After pancakes and rhubarb-jam and milk, and such confusions of words that only a little sense emerges, they want to be outside in the sunshine.

There are butterflies and birds and waves, and wild flowers among the green grass.

The children from the city laugh and shout in a distant field. A dog barks.

The grandmother gathers the dishes to the sink. The pancakes have been eaten, every one. The jam pot has been scoured clean. 'I keep forgetting how hungry bairns get,' she says.

She gathers the dazed and battered bluebottle from its window-pane prison into a duster and releases it into the wind. 'Stupid thing,' she says. 'The door was open all the time.'

Sound of a sob at the corner of the house, a weary foot-drag, a sniffle. (The world is full of pain, from infancy to age.)

Roger stands at the corner of the house, intent on stones. The day has been cruel to Roger.

The grandmother probes, gently, the source of the trouble. Was it Glen, the dog of Smedhurst? 'Glen barks, and jumps up, but he likes bairns. Glen's an excitable dog. I'll take you to Smedhurst tomorrow. We'll make friends with Glen.'

Sam and Margaret are a mile away, on the hillside. Their voices come, green and clear, mixed with bleatings of sheep.

'Tell me this, grandma, were you ever a little girl?'

'Oh yes, I was, a long, long time ago.'

'Where did you stay then, when you were little?'

'I stayed in this very house where we are now.'

'In Inquoy?'

'Yes, indeed, and my own father and grandmother were born and lived here before me.'

'That must be my great-great-grandmother. What was her name?'

'She was called Betsy. I remember her. She had cheeks like apples.'

'Can I have another bit of your toffee, please?'

'Just one more piece. I don't want you to be sick on the first night of your holiday.'

The voices of two children drift up from the shore, remote and blue and cold.

'Are you the oldest lady in the island, grandma?'

'The second oldest. The oldest is Miss Tweeddale. But she's only three months older than me. Miss Tweeddale lives in that big house there against the sky.'

'Did you have a dog like Glen when you were little?'

'When I was peedie — that means small — there was a dog here at Inquoy called Robbie. He was old and lazy. I had a cat for a whole year.'

'What was the cat's name?'

'He was called Fankle. He was a beautiful cat, black as coal. His eyes were like diamonds.'

'Tell me all about Fankle, grandma.'

'Oh dear, that would take all night, and you're far too tired. That's twice now you've yawned. Bedtime for you.'

'I didn't yawn. I was just stretching my mouth. I sometimes do that. Tell me about Fankle.'

'I'll tell you a few things. Fankle was found in the back of a grocery van, among sacks of potatoes. Fankle was a kitten. Mr Strynd found him. Mr Strynd was the general merchant in those days, a long time ago. He's dead now.'

'Did Mr Strynd not want to keep Fankle?'

'Oh no. Mr Strynd hated cats.'

'How did you come to own Fankle, grandma?'

'Mr Strynd said, if I didn't take Fankle, he would drown Fankle in the millpond.'

'That was a terrible thing to say!'

'Wasn't it terrible? So I took Fankle home to Inquoy, that same day.'

'Did Fankle like being in this house?'

'Oh yes, he loved it. Well, most of the time. Sometimes he was in trouble. He couldn't resist fish. He would steal a fish from under your nose.'

'Did you give him a row then?'

'Not me. My mother would give him a row. That's your great-grandma. Fankle was scared whenever she shouted at him. She had a very sharp tongue. Fankle would leap in the air with terror. Fankle would cringe in the corner. Sometimes she would flick him with a dish towel.'

'You must have been very angry with him sometimes when he was bad.'

'Well, he sometimes disappeared for days on end. Then, when he came home at last, I'd give him a piece of my mind.'

'Fankle must have been a rather bad cat.'

'Oh no. Not at all. Certainly not. Most of the time he was good. He was very wise. He was the wisest cat I ever saw.'

'What did the wise cat do all day?'

'Well, he drank three saucers of milk a day. He got a dish with bits of fish on it. Not always fish – sometimes chopped liver, or chicken giblets. He slept a lot of the time in front of the fire. In summer he slept in the sun. He slept under the teacher's desk in the school.'

'Not much fun, just eating and sleeping, grandma.'

'There's another enormous yawn! Bed for you, my boy.'

'I was stretching my mouth. I don't think I'd like a stupid cat that only ate and slept.'

'Ah but, Roger, you never saw Fankle catching the rat! That was something. A great monster of a grey rat, as big as himself. That rat, it destroyed everything my mother did, one summer. It even ate her knitting. She was so annoyed she got asthma. She didn't know what to do. Fankle saved the day. Fankle hunted the brute down.'

'What else did Fankle hunt?'

'Well, birds, sometimes. Starlings and sparrows. Once he tried to eat Mrs Crag's budgie. That was the wickedest thing he ever attempted. We won't speak about Fankle and the birds.'

'What happened to Fankle in the end?'

'What happens to all of us, he died. He was run over.'

'How was he run over?'

'Fankle was crossing the road one day. Round the corner came Mr Strynd's grocery van. Mr Strynd was in a hurry that day. He had a box of eggs and a box of cheese to put on board the *Thor*. *Thor* was the name of the steamer that went between the island and the town. Mr Strynd was late that day. The steamer was due to leave in five minutes. Round the corner came that old rusty chariot, in a cloud of dust and fumes. Fankle had no chance. Of course I knew nothing about it. I was at school. I remember, we were reading *Robinson Crusoe* in the school that afternoon. I've never liked *Robinson Crusoe* since that day. Well, I came home, and there was a small black heap on the doorstep, with streaks of grey and red on it. It took me a while to recognize Fankle. I thought at first he'd been hunting in the quarry and was asleep. It took me longer to realize Fankle was dead. When I saw my mother crying at the sink, I knew the thing on the doorstep was Fankle, and that Fankle wouldn't be telling any more stories again.'

'Did you cry, grandma?'

'Yes, of course I did. I cried all that night. I was still crying in my sleep, my mother said.'

'Poor grandma.'

'Poor you. If you stretch your mouth any more, you'll crack your face. Off with the shoes first. It's time your brother and sister were in. It's beginning to get dark.'

'I wish I'd known Fankle.'

'I have a photograph of him. I'll show you Fankle's photo in the morning. It's too dark now. He's buried under the cabbage patch, in a shoe box. Now, your jersey.'

'Did you cry for days and weeks, grandma?'

'No, just that one night. Next morning I realized that Fankle wasn't dead at all.'

'The van went over him. He was put in a shoe box. He was buried under the cabbages.'

'He was. But you see, precious, cats have nine lives. And as far as I could gather, Fankle still had three to go.'

'Where is he now then?'

'I wish I knew. Some amazing place, you may be sure of that. Fankle always went where there was glamour and power and excitement. The thing that amazes me, Roger, is why he ever chose to come to a quiet poor place like this, and live for a year with a plain girl like Jenny. . . . You won't be getting a bath tonight, you're too tired. Now then, where are those pyjamas?'

The old woman is aware of two young flushed darkling faces at the window. The child sees nothing. He does not hear the twilight and star laughter. He is asleep, in his white pyjamas, curled up in his grandma's strawback chair.

Sam and Margaret come in.

'Who's Jenny, grandma?' says Margaret. 'Did you have trouble with that little wretch? Has he been snivelling for a long time? Little sniveller, frightened of a dog! I heard you saying a girl's name, grandma — Jenny.'

'Roger has been a very good boy. I'm going to put him to his bed now. There's scones and raspberry jam for your supper.'

'Oh, goody gumdrops,' says Sam. 'I'm *starving*.'

'Jenny? Jenny is the name of a girl that used to stay in this island — oh, a long long time ago.'

'We always get a story, grandma, before we go to sleep. Don't we, Margaret?'

'Your mouth is all red with raspberry jam, glutton.'

'No, but don't we get a story at bedtime?'

'Sometimes.'

'*Always.* We always get a night story, grandma. Mum tells us a story, or she reads a story. I don't think I could go to sleep if I didn't get a story.'

'It's many a long day since I told a story, child. When I was a girl, like Margaret, my life was all stories. Not now. I'm just an old woman who potters about.'

'Grandma, listen to Roger snoring next door. Give him a row for that in the morning.'

'A story. A story. I demand a story.'

'Well, I may try. I'll light this candle first. Candle-light makes a story sound better. Are you ready? There was this little boy called Lentil-soup and one day when he was out picking blackberries on the hill he saw a small green man standing before him. Lentil-soup knew that the creature was a fairy. The fairy said to Lentil-soup, 'Give us a few of your blackberries to make a pie." Lentil-soup answered —'

'Is it going to be a fairy story, grandma?'

'Of course it is, you idiot. Didn't you hear grandma mentioning a fairy? Don't interrupt.'

'I don't want fairy stories. What do you think I am, a kid? None of that fairy rubbish for me.'

'What kind of story do you want then, Sam?'

'Pay no attention to him, grandma. I'm going to write and tell mum about him in the morning. I will.'

'I like science fiction. I like stories about space flight and the stars.'

'Mercy, bairn, what does an old woman know about such things!'

'Just try, grandma. Then I'll be good and get your messages from the village in the morning.'

'He won't, grandma. He's the biggest liar. He breaks every promise he ever makes.'

'Science fiction. There's been enough science fiction happening in this island since I was a peedie lass. That oil rig out there. The uranium mine on the other side of the hill. Men dropping into the sea with globes on their heads. Let me tell you this, science has made a fine mess of the island. I know you like coming here for your summer holiday. But you don't have the freedom I had when I was your age. Fumes and dust everywhere. The wind here used to be like crystal. From the top of the cliff you could see right down to the ocean floor, it was so clear. Now it's all mucky and putrid. Oh, I could go on and on!'

'The story, grandma.'

'Grandma, do you think you could possibly tell a story about the moon? That would be space fiction. I saw a new moon over the hill tonight.'

'Perhaps I could.'

'If you tell a story about the moon, I'll wash the dishes every day. I will.'

'The moon. Let me see. There must be hundreds of stories about the moon.'

'One'll do for a start.'

'I suppose you think, Sammy, the moon's a dead cold lump of rock. That's where you're wrong. As a matter of fact, the moon is inhabited by marvellous animals, such as were only found on earth in the morning of time. Then they roamed free and happy among the other earth animals — among the horses, whales, wolves, cats, eagles, reindeer, bears. But those other animals were clever, very clever. As soon as man appeared on the scene, they saw what would be what. The horses, bears, cats, etcetera, were very curious when they first set eyes on man. "Dear me, look at this," they said to one another. "Isn't it quaint? Just look at it, going about on two legs, and its other two legs high up and moving about in the air. Well, all we animals will have to try to be good to this new creature. Let's help him in any way we can. Let's try to make him at home on the earth. He won't be able to do much by

110

himself, will he? We'll go and make friends with him now."

'So all the animals went up to man and stood round about him and bade him welcome to earth, in their various voices. Elephant trumpeted, dog barked, seal grunted, horse whinnied, gull screamed, fish made a little water song too fine for the ears of man to hear.

'Man said to his wife and children, "Look at all the creatures who have come to help us. We can't let an opportunity like this slip. . . ." He went into his house of leaves and came out with a bow and arrow and shot the dove who was sitting on a branch. Down fell dove, dead, with the arrow right through him. "Make pigeon pie," said man to his blunt-nosed wife. "I fancy pigeon pie for my supper." So the wife took the dead bird indoors and lit a fire. The animals were very puzzled by this behaviour. Weapons, little cluster of flames — they looked at each other in wonderment. Man said, "You there, sheep, you're to come round here tomorrow morning first thing. Understand, all of you, I'm master here now. I want some of that wool of yours, sheep, for a coat. I don't know what I can do with you, lion. Cow, there's better drink in those buttercup-tasting udders of yours than's in the well. I'm going to tether you at the end of my house. Listen, worm, I'm going to use you to catch fish — isn't that a good idea! (I smell the pigeon in the pot now — delicious. My wife is getting to be a good cook.) Cat, I want you to come and play with my little boy. Horse — now let me think — I've been digging the earth and sowing seed — very hard work. The other night I got an idea. Why not have a sharp curve of wood dragged along the earth, and then sow the whole field in a morning? Horse, you're the very one to do that. Report here, horse, on the first day of spring. You've been romping idly about in the wind and sun too long. . . ." At this point man spied pig cavorting round a stone. He fitted another arrow into his bow and shot pig through its fat jolly neck. Pig gave a little grunt and a twitch and it died. "I'll salt it," said man. "Must think of the future.

I'll get some good chops out of pig next winter. . . ."

'The animals were amazed. They said goodnight in their various ways to man and trooped back to their meeting place in the forest clearing. There was a large deep lake there too so that the whales and other fish could attend.

'Lion said, "I just don't know. I have never seen cold brutality like that in all my time under the sun. Certainly man is clever. He can do things that we can't do. He has even made fire — that terror — work for him. Perhaps it's our duty to help him in any way we can. I would welcome some opinions on this rather serious business. I tell you frankly that my immediate inclination tonight, when I saw first pigeon and then pig slaughtered in that dreadful way, was to tear man to pieces."

' "No," said horse. "We must indeed help him. I've promised to drag a plough for him, and I will, as soon as it's spring. This creature has more in him, in some ways, than all the rest of us put together. He will, I know, do great things on the earth. In a sense the earth has been holding its breath, for thousands of years, waiting for the coming of man."

' "He is very beautiful," said peacock, "if you look at him in a certain slant of light."

'At this point Himp-hunk came forward to address the assembly. (Himp-hunk is an animal you've never seen.) Himp-hunk spoke very gravely. "What we have seen today, fellow animals," he said, "is only the beginning. This new creature has shown us what he can do, and what he means to do. He has no intention of joining in the beautiful dance of creation, with us other animals, and with the stars and plants and grains of dust and sun and moon. No, he intends to dominate creation. He will use every means in his power to do just that. He will use us, just as he uses the tree to make his weapons and houses and fires. He will go so far as to destroy us, if he thinks it necessary."

' "Hear hear," said Jimp-jack, who was a creature half-fish and half-bird. "I have never once been frightened on this planet until today, when I saw what man could do with his bow and arrow."

'Then Wurton lumbered to his feet. He was huger than a gorilla, but he had a face gentle as a flower. "Brother Himp-hunk has spoken well and wisely," he said. "This new creature will ruin the beautiful song of creation. We animals are not cruel unnecessarily — we only kill when we are hungry, and then it is a clean acceptable death we deal. My plan is this, that we surround the house of man tonight, and then when he comes out of his door in the morning, to stand in the sun with his wife and child, we fall on the family and kill them with as little fuss as possible."

'The little snail said, in his silver voice, "Man is part of the dance too. In time we will understand him. Then all will be well."

'The silkworm said, "I will give him beautiful coats."

'Swintock (who hopped on one leg and had seven eyes) said, "Man is a murderer. Blot him out."

'The debate went on all night. In the end it got fierce and bitter, a thing that had never happened before; the speeches of the animals were normally all wonder and delight.

'In the end they decided to vote on the question as to whether man was to be welcomed, or destroyed. There were seventy-eight votes in favour of man, and twenty-six against. Those against included Himp-hunk, Jimp-jack, Wurton, Swintock, Syblick, Garter-grace, Airy-tong, Slumberlite, Graycroke, Assiepat, Cloud-cleaver, Delver, Dreamdinge, Fenderley, Essywhat, Ragbeam, Goldboy, Mountain-spinner, Tenpole, Swartfish, Andrake, Ally-bally, Kirstane, Swaylpot, Toelash, Twinklebream, Papy-ruck, Denplane, and Cat.'

'Cat?' says Sam.

'Cat,' says the old lady. 'C — A — T.'

'Cat,' says Margaret. 'Are you deaf, Sam? Grandma said cat.'

'Those anti-man animals retired to another part of the forest to consider their position.

'For a week they thrashed the matter out. The more they went into the question, the more dreadful and sinister the shadow that man threw over the beautiful earth. At the end of the week they decided that it would be unendurable to share the planet with a cold-blooded murderer like man. They decided to emigrate *en masse*. Long they debated which star or planet to settle in. Himp-hunk was all in favour of going to the golden castle of the sun. Swintock thought it would be good fun to glide and swim and dance forever through the streams of the merry dancers. But at last common-sense prevailed. They decided that the moon, the nearest heavenly body, was to be their future home.'

('And how,' says Sam, 'would they get to the moon? There were no rockets or space ships in them days.'

'Shut up, just listen,' says Margaret.)

'I'll tell you how they got to the moon. They waited until the full moon was just touching the hill out there one night. Then, one after the other, they leapt and flew and clambered into that round silver house.

'The moon animals live there quite happily. The only times they are troubled are when, every hundred years or so, Graycroke, who has an eye more powerful than any telescope ever built, looks at the earth and tells the other moon animals what he sees. Then a sadness falls on the moon creatures. What they feared in the beginning is coming to pass, faster and faster. Man is trying to dominate the whole of creation, with the greatest cruelty, unscrupulousness, and cunning. In particular — they realize this with growing horror — the animals they have left behind on earth, the friends of man, are being enslaved and destroyed.

'Graycroke looked once through his enormous crystal eye. He said, "I see lion. Lion is locked in a cage, in a city zoo, thousands of miles from the desert. A man comes from time to time and feeds that noble, powerful creature with a hunk of dead horse."

'Graycroke said, again, "I see elephant. Elephant is dragging logs through a jungle clearing. He stumbles. Man has worked him to the bone. In the end, the beautiful curves of ivory are drawn from his earth-fast head."

'Graycroke said, again, "I see blue whale. Blue whale is stuck full with harpoons. He is staining the sea with his rich oil and blood. Soon the ocean will be empty of blue whale forever."

'Graycroke said, once more, "I see cow. Cow has dowered man for many a summer with milk and butter and cheese. There she hangs, cut into red sections, each dreadful piece hanging from a steel hook at a wall reeking with blood."

'Graycroke cried out in pain, "I see rabbit now. Rabbit is coming out of his house under the sand. Man has injected a dreadful sickness into rabbit. Now rabbit blunders among the dunes, blind and deaf and suppurating. His death is a lingering agony."

'All this the moon animals got to know through the cloud-piercing eye of Graycroke, as the years and centuries went past. The fact of man filled many of them with burning rage. What could they do? What ought they to do? I don't know how many solemn debates were held in the moon parliament. At length, in the year 2001, a critical debate was announced by Swintock, the speaker of the moon parliament that year: *That this House proceeds forthwith to ordain and order, by all means possible, the early destruction of the planet Earth; since one species on the said planet Earth, man, has from his creation committed sundry grave outrages, woundings, and death upon his fellow creatures (not to speak of his despoiling of minerals, and his pollutions of air and earth and water, so that whole regions of the beautiful Earth — our former home — are no longer fit to live in; and now, worse threatens, in that man is looking outwards into space, for the purpose of extending his cruel empire there, and has even made sundry landings on the crust of our enchanting home, the moon: we therefore now solemnly resolve to eliminate this canker called man from the universe, till no trace of him or his kindred remain....*

'You know of course that the moon regulates the ebb and flow of our seas. The moon-animals have long had control of the enormous magnets that operate the earth-tides. It was quite within their power to pull out the flood-levers to their fullest extent; in which case – as in the days of Noah – the solid earth would become in an instant a saturated dripping sponge in which everything, from a sandfly to the yeti on the slope of Mount Everest, would be drowned.

'One of the moon animals especially, Himp-hunk, took to prowling about the doors of the chamber that housed the tidal magnets. How Himp-hunk longed to get his paws on those flood levers!

'Every animal, as he spoke in the debate, was listened to with earnest close attention.

'Man the destroyer. . . . Man the murderer. . . . Perfidious Man. . . . These were the commonest phrases used by speaker after speaker.

'As the debate grew to an end, it seemed that the vote would be overwhelmingly in favour of the swift drowning and destruction of Earth.

'Finally all the animals had spoken with the exception of Cat.'

'Cat,' says Sam. 'Cat? Cat is one of the earth animals. Everybody knows that.'

'That's where you're wrong,' says grandma. 'Cat belongs to the two worlds, earth and moon. Cat can go from one to the other in a twinkling. Have you ever looked in a cat's eyes, how they change like the moon from crescent to full? That's the sign of a moon animal. The eyes of all the moon animals are like that, they change like the moon itself.'

'Tell me then — how does Cat get from earth to moon and back again? Does he have his own private space ship?'

'Grandma, why don't you tell Sam, once and for all, to shut his blooming cheeky mouth!'

'This is what happens, Sam. Cat waits till the moon is balanced for a second on the crest of the hill out there — then he leaps softly on to the silver threshold. It's as simple as that, Sam.

'At last Cat caught the speaker's eye. He got slowly to his feet. There wasn't much point in him speaking, really. The moon animals had already arrived at their decision.

'Cat spoke slowly at first. He agreed that there was much evil and destructiveness in man. Man (he said) was unique in that he actually warred with himself. Alone of all the animals, man, on the slightest whim or excuse, would turn upon his fellows and wound, maim, enslave, kill. Also, man always found a noble word, such as "patriotism" or "progress" or "freedom", to excuse the butchery. Truly man was a frightening species. "And yet," said Cat, "we only see man and his works from a great distance, through the powerful crystal eye of Graycroke. You moon animals get only a general view of the situation on earth. But I, Cat, live half my time on earth and half my time here on the moon. I do not have an abstract view of *man*. I have instead some knowledge of individual men and women and boys and girls. They have names. They laugh and cry. They visit each other with gifts and gossip. When they are young, when they are in love, when they are making something and enjoying their work, everything they do and say is wonderful. None of the other animals, I think, has such beauty then. Let me remind you of this — even on our first acquaintance with man, when he murdered dove and pig, we realized all the same that he had entrancing possibilities in him; more than any other creature.

' "If those possibilities come to fruition, fellow moon animals, man will make of earth a place of unimaginable

117

beauty, bounty, wisdom. On that day, there will be a treaty signed. Men will be fully accepted into the dance of creation. Animals and men will love one another at last, as they were meant to do."

'Cat then went on to mention Orpheus, St Francis, Robert Burns as human beings who had loved in their day the entire animal creation. There were thousands of good people on earth like them. But if, tomorrow morning, those torrents of water were to be unleashed, all that hope and promise would be lost.

'Himp-hunk shouted from the other side of the chamber, "Bunk! Humbug! Earthshine! Don't listen to that cat. He's a traitor, I know it. He's on their side. Cat is no friend of the moon animals. Cat spends half his time at the hateful fires of man. Sit down, traitor, hypocrite! You won't change us now, Cat, with your eloquent miaows and purrings."

'The Speaker of the assembly, Swintock (he who hopped on one leg and had seven eyes) rebuked Himp-hunk. He ordered him sharply to sit down. No one had interrupted Himp-hunk's speech. Cat was in a good position to provide information to the assembly; he indeed knew man more intimately than any of the others there present. If Cat could convince the assembly that there was a hope of man's eventual reconciliation, no doubt the assembly would think about the matter again. But, Mr Speaker warned Cat, no vague legends about Orpheus and St Francis – beautiful though they were – were likely to convince the delegates. Was there a red loving heart, or a cold grey stone, in the middle of man's body? That was the kernel of the matter.

'The Speaker ordered Cat to proceed with his speech. . .

('Cat won't blab on much longer, I hope,' says Sam. 'I'm longing for the levers to be pulled. I'm eager for the end of the world.'

'Carry on, grandma. Never mind him.')

'Cat, after Himp-hunk's angry interruption, went on

118

with his speech. "Pardon, Mr Speaker," he said. "Up to
now I've been rather longwinded, I admit. I would like to
end my speech by telling this assembly a few stories about
men and women and children, and some of the things I
have learned about them. I hope you will hear, in the tales
I am going to tell you now, the true heart-beat of humanity;
which will still be sounding when all that was evil is
mingled in dust and ashes."

' "Hear-hear!" shouted the moon parliament. (There's
nothing moon animals like better than stories.)

'The moon animals heard then, from the mouth of Cat,
the story of the good ship *Esmeralda*, and how, in the
midst of much that was violent and treacherous, the virtue
of faithfulness shone out in the person of a certain sailor
called Tomas and a little black cabin-boy, Mint. . . . At the
conclusion, the moon animals murmured their admiration;
all except Himp-hunk, who grunted nastily.

'There was a great deal of laughter in the assembly as
the second story unfolded. It was all about a melancholy
old lady called Mrs Martin and her fat good son who
seemed to be killing himself with too much cherry-cake.
("They are rather touching and ridiculous, human beings,"
murmured Jimp-jack. Himp-hunk snarled.)

'Cat's third story mentioned, incidentally, an Egyptian
princess whose name meant "she-who-will-bake-cakes-for-
the-poor". "I see," murmured Slumberlite, the moon
animal who consisted of six interlocking wheels of various
sizes, "that pity and kindness are a part of some human
beings, at least. . . ." Himp-hunk covered his burning eyes.

'Cat paused, and took a sip of milk from the glass on the
table in front of him. His voice was by now a bit hoarse
with speaking. . . . He next went on to speak about children in an island — how their limbs were sun-dark in
summer, how their cheeks were apple-bright in the snow,
how one of them wanted to take a snowman home for a
bowl of soup beside the fire. ("The young ones are certainly very beautiful," said Syblic, half-butterfly and half-

badger. "A pity they have to grow up. They're not *entirely* wicked, if that's the way they begin. . . ." (Himp-hunk gave a bitter laugh.)

'Perhaps the story that moved the assembly most was the one about a poor river girl, Bat-ye, who made beautiful things of reeds, then silk, and in the end became an Empress. But she never forgot the river-people; she made her love known to them though they thought she was lost, or stolen, or drowned, long since. ("If love like this wins through in the end," said Wurton, who was huger than a gorilla but whose face was gentle as a flower, "then man might be worthy at last of a place in the universe. I think it's worth trying. I think we should give him another chance." Himp-hunk wept, and shook his paws in the air with rage.)

'"I have finished," said Fankle. "I thank the moon parliament for its patience. I recommend man to your mercy."

'The vote was twenty in favour of giving man another thousand years to prove himself a good citizen of the universe, and seven against. All the crystal bells of the moon rang out in celebration of a marvellous debate. But Himp-hunk, where was he? Himp-hunk was not to be found, either in the voting lobbies or sitting asleep (as was his habit in the afternoon) under the Himp-hunk tree. They found him, not a moment too soon, among the underground tide-controls, fumbling dementedly with the levers. He was dragged away before he could saturate Earth with drowning and death. He was put into a rest-home for a year; and he came out a very much improved animal, though he could never be got to say a single good word about man: not to his dying day.'

'What about Jenny? Did Fankle, or whatever the cat's name was, have nothing to say about Jenny in his speech?'

'He would have, Margaret, only he thought his speech had gone on too long already. There was nothing special about Jenny anyway. The moon animals wouldn't have been very impressed with a plain country girl like Jenny.'

'What's this? Is the story finished? Do you mean to say, grandma, the flood magnets were never switched on? What a swizz of a story!'

'I liked it anyway. I did, grandma.'

'I see four eyes stuck with syrup. The candle's been out for half-an-hour. Bedtime. One thing for sure, your story tomorrow night, and every other night, will be shorter and sweeter.'

The old lady is alone beside the fire. The dark house is possessed by three regular breath-rhythms, delicate and pure.

Jenny's grandchildren are asleep in various corners of Inquoy.

CATCH A KELPIE

If you enjoyed this book
you would probably enjoy our other Kelpies.

Here's a complete list to choose from:

for further details of Canongate Kelpies write to
Canongate Publishing, 17 Jeffrey Street, Edinburgh

THE WELL AT THE WORLD'S END

Folk Tales of Scotland

This magical little book contains thrity-five folk and fairy tales, legends and some poems from almost every corner of Scotland, including Orkney and Shetlands, the West Highlands and the Lowlands. Some are taken from Gaelic translations, the richest area in Scottish folklore.

So intrigued were the authors by the stories they gathered, they decided to present them in English for easier reading for the wide audience they deserve rather than in dialect.

But it is the stories themselves, weird, comic and heroic, that make the book and invite us to live in a world where fairies, princes and monsters are a normal part of everyday life.

Norah and William Montgomerie

THE STORY OF RANALD

After the battle of Culloden, Ranald Macdonald and his family are forced to flee their homes to escape the barbarities of the cruel English soliders under the command of 'Butcher Cumberland'.

With his father held prisoner in Carlisle, Ranald finds his former life as a carefree young boy must change if he is to protect and assist his womenfolk in their perilous quest for freedom.

This is a true story based on Ranald's own account written in 1749, two years after his escape. It gives a rare insight as to how it must have been to leave a beloved home and country as a fugitive never to return.

Griselda Gifford

ROBBIE

Every morning Robbie hurtles down the rough winding road to the school bus, cheered on by his schoolfriends. Every afternoon his grandfather meets him when he comes home, and, as the the two explore the Fife countryside the old man tells the boy about 'the old times'.

In these stories Emil Pacholek vividly describes Robbie's life as he grows up on a farm in the 1950s. He tells of fun, adventures and triumphs — and of Robbie's sadness. The old traditions, like the village 'Harvest Home', survive, but signs of the modern world are all around and the Hawker Hunters scream through the sky from the military air station at Leuchars. Robbie's life changes too, as he loses one companion and cements his friendship with another.

Emil Pacholek

THE MAGIC WALKING STICK

Home from school for his half-term holiday, Bill acquires a walking-stick from a little wizened old man. He soon discovers that this stick has magic properties, capable of transporting him to any part of the world he wishes.

After some experiments and dangerous visits to such places as the Soloman Islands, the elephants' grave in Africa and a dramatic rescue trip in the Sahara desert, Bill discovers that there are two such magic sticks in the world. One is for gallivanting and amusement, the other for chivalrous deeds. Misuse of either stick would result in its disappearance.

Which one does Bill have?

No-one can tell an adventure story like John Buchan and in this tale his imagination and sense of excitement know no bounds as his hero performs daring deeds in the most unlikely places.

John Buchan